KT-234-970

2019

Old Pals Act

Old Pals Act

JAMES PATTINSON

ROBERT HALE · LONDON

© James Pattinson 2001
First published in Great Britain 2001

ISBN 0 7090 6807 7

Robert Hale Limited
Clerkenwell House
Clerkenwell Green
London EC1R 0HT

2 4 6 8 10 9 7 5 3 1

Typeset by
Derek Doyle & Associates, Liverpool.
Printed in Great Britain by
St Edmundsbury Press, Bury St Edmunds, Suffolk.
Bound by Woolnough Bookbinding Ltd.

Contents

Chapter One

OLD ACQUAINTANCE

There was a woman standing at the door of his flat when Brady returned to it. She had her back to him and she was sounding the buzzer.

'It's no use doing that,' he said. 'There's no one at home.'

She took her finger off the button then and turned to face him and said: 'Oh, there you are, Steve. This is the second time I've called. Where have you been?'

She sounded rather put out about it, as though she felt that he should have had the decency to be at home when she visited him, whenever it might be.

He saw now who this visitor was. He had suspected it was her even when he had had only the rear view. Now he was certain.

'My God!' he said. 'Linda! Well, well, well! This is a surprise. Long time, no see.'

It had in fact been several years. With a quick piece of mental calculation he reckoned she must now be on the wrong side of thirty-five – though not by much. Well, he was that age himself, so she had to be as well. The gap would not have altered with the passing of time.

But she did not look that old. The hair, worn rather longer now than he remembered it, was still as black and glossy as a raven's wing, with no hint of any tell-tale grey in it. She seemed to be keeping the wrinkles at bay too; and those eyes and that figure! His pulse rate was going up by the minute just at the sight of her. How had he ever been so stupid as to lose touch with her? He must really have been out of his mind.

But of course it had not really been he who had made the break. When the Wall came down there seemed to be a lack of jobs for her lot to pass his way. And he had never been really keen on taking the jobs she pushed on to him anyway. Espionage was not truly his line of country; he was just co-opted now and then when the department she worked for happened to be in need of an auxiliary to take on a sticky assignment for which none of the regulars was at that moment available. At least, so they said. Though in fact he had a shrewd suspicion that they regarded him as expendable material and were frequently a trifle surprised when he survived and turned up to claim his pay – such as it was.

There had been one particularly hair-raising piece of business which had involved getting across the border between East and West Germany. It had been a veritable obstacle course in those days, what with barbed-wire entanglements and minefields and tripwires and electrified fences and ditches with spikes in them and guard dogs and watch-towers and the devil and all besides. He had had a guide of course, a man named Karl, a proper nut-case who had made the crossing on one or two previous occa-sions and lived to tell the tale. Not any more, though. That time there had been a betrayal and he had got himself blown to pieces by a fiendish explosive device on the last fence. In a way it might have been said that he had given his life for Brady, because if he had not triggered the device Brady himself might have done so with equally fatal consequences. But as it was he had made it to safety on the other side, where amongst others Linda Manning had been waiting for him.

They had wanted to get him back alive from that mission, not because of any great concern for him but because of a little piece of the latest type of armour plating for tanks that had been developed in an East German research establishment. This sample of the new material had, unknown to him, been implanted in his body, making him temporarily a valuable pawn in the Cold War.

But that was all years ago, and now the two halves of Germany had joined up again and people could come and go as they pleased, with Checkpoint Charlie nothing more than a bitter memory.

Not that he had ever been back to take a look at things over there now that he was free to do so without risk to life and limb. Nor had he paid any return visits to Russia or any of the other former communist states where he had taken an unwilling hand in the espionage game. Even now he would not have felt truly at ease over there. He would have been half expecting the hand on his shoulder, the prod in the back with a cold hard object that just had to be the muzzle of a self-loading pistol, the demand to see his papers which he knew were forgeries.

There had been a few compensations for all the unpleasantness he had to accept on these expeditions, and all of these as far as he could recall were female. He had almost forgotten their names. There was a Polish girl, very lovely. Paula, that was it. She had accompanied him on a hectic journey in Middle Europe, and years later she had turned up again in Antwerp. But in the end she had drowned in the North Sea, which was one hell of a way to go.

There was another girl in Bulgaria who had helped him; but they had both been caught trying to find a way across the border into Macedonia, and he had eventually found himself floating on a raft in the Black Sea after the ship that was to have carried him to Russia had blown up and sunk. He had been picked up by a Turkish freighter, but he never saw the girl again; never knew what happened to her. And he had after all been nothing but a damned stalking-horse sent out to take the heat off a regular agent who was being installed to take the place of one who had come to a sticky end; which of course nobody saw fit to tell him until later.

Another time he and Linda had travelled to Moscow posing as man and wife. There had been an idyllic interlude by a lakeside in Finland, just the two of them in a log cabin for a while. But that had ended all too soon because of some treachery by a man named Stewart Cobb, and they had been fortunate to escape from Russia with their lives. There was some business in Central America too; where a girl named Teresa had given him quite a bit of assistance when he most needed it. That had been a courier job, which of course went wrong, with an earthquake adding one more complication to the operation.

Thoughts of these long past assignments flashed into his mind as he stood looking at Linda and wondering just what had brought her back into his life and whether he ought to be glad or otherwise. There had been a time when her appearance on his doorstep would have brought a feeling of apprehension mingled with the pleasure, a shiver down the spine. Because invariably she would bring with her news of a new assignment, which, despite assurances to the contrary, would nevertheless involve him in some very risky business indeed.

But of course all that sort of thing was past and done with.

The Cold War was history and there was no possibility that this visit of the delightful Miss Manning, if that still was her name, was anything more than a social call on an old friend and colleague and one-time lover.

Was there?

Finally, it was she who broke the silence, bringing to an end that brief interval of mutual and mute appraisal which had followed their initial exchange of greetings.

'Well, Steve,' she said, 'don't you think we might go inside? Unless you have some objection. Have you?'

'Why no, Of course not. I'm just getting over the shock of seeing you again. Stunned me for the moment.'

'Shock? That sounds as if you found it unpleasant seeing me once more after all this time. Am I such an ogre?'

'Not at all. Far from it.' He was fishing the key out of his pocket, fitting it in the lock. 'Maybe surprise would have been a better word to use. Pleasant surprise of course. How could it be otherwise?'

He opened the door and ushered her in, closing it behind them.

'Let me take your coat.'

She was wearing a white trench-coat. She got herself out of it, and he took it from her and hung it on a peg in the small entrance hall before showing the way into the living-room. She stood quite still just inside and took a careful look at it. Brady watched her, waiting for the verdict.

'Well,' she said at last, 'it's certainly better than the old place. I can see you've come up in the world.'

'A little,' he admitted. Though of course it did not take much to be an advance on that shabby little pad he had occupied in the old days. There was nothing luxurious about his present abode, but at least there was more elbow-room in it and it was decently furnished in a plain and simple style. 'Do you like it?'

'It's not bad,' she said. 'Not bad at all. How come? Did you have a win on the Lottery?'

'Not a chance. Fact is, I don't do the Lottery. The odds are rather poor, you know. Horse-racing is a better bet.'

'Don't tell me a rich aunt died and left you a packet.'

'I haven't got any rich aunts,' Brady said. 'Dead or alive. Now you may find this hard to believe, but I got a job. In the antiques business.'

'I see,' she said. And he thought she seemed rather disappointed. 'Isn't that the line you were in when we first met?'

'It was. But I was self-employed then. Or perhaps I should say self-unemployed, since I never really made a go of it?'

'And now you're back in it with a solid job?'

'Well, no; actually not. I've had the push. Business is poor, so they let me go. That's the way they put it; as if I'd been straining at the leash to break free and they'd yielded to my pleading.'

'So what are you doing now?'

'Taking a look around.'

'And waiting for something to turn up, like Mr Micawber.'

'If you care to put it that way.'

'But nothing actually in sight?'

'No.'

'In that case,' she said, 'this could be your lucky day.'

Brady looked at her with some suspicion. 'Now I wonder,' he said, 'just why that remark gives me a faintly queasy feeling in the pit of the stomach.'

'I can't imagine,' she answered, without the least hint of a smile. 'As I recall, I've often given you the chance to earn some badly needed hard cash. Isn't that so?'

Brady admitted the undoubted truth of this. 'But at what cost, Linda, at what cost?'

'Oh, the odd scar or two; a certain amount of discomfort now and then. But in the service of Queen and Country, what are they?'

'A mere nothing if you say it quickly. Similarly all the wear and tear on the nervous system and the occasional infliction of a spot of physical or mental torture in the effort to extract secret information, which, I may say, I was never in a position to divulge, since I had not been trusted with it in the first place.'

'Really, Steve,' she said, 'you're beginning to sound very querulous. And it was all so long ago. I hate to think how long. And besides, there were some good things too, weren't there? Or have you forgotten?'

He grinned at her. 'As if I could forget! Ever.'

'Now look,' she said. 'Why are we standing here like a pair of stuffed dummies? What I'm dying for is a cup of that famous Darjeeling tea you used to make. Do you still have some?'

'So you remember that,' he said. And it pleased him to learn that she had not forgotten.

'Of course. And whenever I drink a cup of it now I think of you. Its very aroma brings back the memories.'

'Sweet memories?'

'Oh, very sweet.'

He wondered whether she was kidding; just saying this to flatter him and soften him up for some purpose yet to be revealed.

'Well,' he said, 'in this establishment it's always teatime. So I'll go and brew up. And maybe then it'll really be like the old times.'

'The good old times?'

'Oh, sure, The best of them, Linda, the very best.'

Chapter Two

INVITATION

She followed him into the kitchen and remarked that this too was a great deal better than the poky little hole that had served as one in the old place.

'But I see you've still got the same pot.'

'You bet. Wouldn't taste the same out of anything else.'

It was brown earthenware, slightly chipped. Brady spooned tea from a tin caddy while the water heated in an electric jug-kettle.

'The same old pot and, as you will observe, no tea-bags.'

'In some ways, Steve,' she said, 'you're a complete stick-in-the-mud.'

'Why change for the worse? Not all progress is an improvement.'

'True. But we can't stop it, you know.'

'Unfortunately.'

They drank the tea and ate chocolate biscuits sitting at the kitchen table.

'This is so nice,' Linda said. 'I can't think why we ever lost touch.'

Brady reflected that she knew very well. He had been of use to her for a while, and there had even been occasions when he had thought about marriage. But it had never been on, of course. How could he have proposed such a thing when he was living from hand to mouth? She would have ridiculed the idea. Or would she? He would never know now.

'Tell me,' she said. 'Are you living here all alone?'

'Do you see anyone else around?'

'No, but—'

'But you think there may have been someone?'

'The thought had occurred to me.'

'And you're curious?'

'Naturally.'

'Well, I'll tell you. There was someone.'

'But not now?'

'No.'

He had a feeling that she was not displeased to hear this, though she did not say so; and he would have been surprised if she had. She just looked at him and said nothing. But without any prompting he said:

'Her name was Irene.'

'A nice name. You were in love with her?'

'I thought so at one time. I was crazy about her.'

She gave a faint smile. 'As I remember, you always were pretty crazy.'

'I needed to be to take the kind of jobs you handed out to me.'

'That's a matter of opinion. So why did you and Irene split up? Did you have a fight?'

'Nothing so uncivilized. She just told me she considered it was not in her best interests to stick with a man who had lost his job and showed few signs of getting another. You can see that she had a point.'

'Oh yes, from a purely mercenary viewpoint. But what about true love? Didn't that count for anything?'

'In her calculations very little, I imagine.'

'And you? What was your reaction?'

'To be perfectly honest, I wasn't exactly devastated. Things had been turning a bit sour for some time. Frankly, I was quite relieved that it should have ended with so little rancour. No tantrums or anything like that; no recriminations; just a quiet parting of the ways, mutually acceptable.'

'That's the way it should be. But too often isn't.'

He wondered whether she was speaking from experience, and he said: 'How about you? Any man in your life right now?'

She shook her head. 'No. No one. Not in fact since my marriage hit the rocks.'

'So you've been married!'

'Does it surprise you so much?'

It did. But he could see no good reason why it should.

'Anyway, it didn't last long. Not much more than a year. It was a mistake. But we all make mistakes, don't we?'

'I guess we do. I've made plenty. So you're no longer Linda Manning?'

'Yes, I am.'

'You don't use your married name?'

'No.'

'Any particular reason?'

She grimaced. 'A very good one. At least to my mind. It was Potts. Herbert Potts was the man.'

Brady controlled an impulse to laugh, though the mental picture of her as Mrs Herbert Potts made this difficult.

'OK,' she said. 'Laugh if you want to.'

'Nothing was further from my mind.'

'That's a lie of course. But let's skip it.'

'So what went wrong?'

'Just about everything. I suppose we were simply not compatible. Which we discovered very quickly.'

'And I imagine your job must have made things difficult too.'

'What job would that be?'

'Why, with the undercover lot you were working for. The people who used to hand out all the dodgy jobs to yours truly.'

'Oh no,' she said. 'I'd already left them. There was a lot of weeding out when the Cold War ended, you see.'

'And you were one of the weeds?'

'That would be one way of putting it.'

He was relieved to hear this, because there had been a nagging suspicion at the back of his mind that even now, even with the Iron Curtain torn to shreds, she still might possibly be there with the intention of raking him in for a part in one of those operations with the assurance of absolutely no risk attached but which inevitably succeeded in scaring him to hell and back.

'So,' he said, 'what are you doing to pass the time away? Writing your memoirs?'

'Not yet. Some day, maybe. And you'll figure in them. That's a promise. But at the moment I have a job with an outfit called Adsum Worldwide.'

'Never heard of it.'

'I didn't think you would have. It's not on everybody's lips.'

'And what's their line of business?'

'Various.'

'That's a bit vague.'

'Yes, it is, isn't it?'

She nibbled at a biscuit and drank some more tea.

'By the way,' Brady said, 'how did you find me?'

'Oh, I went to the old address, but nobody there seemed to have heard of you. So then I looked in the phone book and there you were, with this address.'

'But there must be loads of Bradys listed.'

'Not so many with the initials S.Z.W.'

'I suppose not.' And he reflected that not many people knew that his names were Stephen Zachariah William. It just showed how intimate he and Linda had been at times in the past, that he should have confided this piece of information to her. It was not something he spread around. Even Irene had never known about the Zachariah. 'Well, it's certainly nice seeing you again, but there's a question that occurs to me.'

'Which is?'

'How come this sudden urge to catch up with me again? Did the thought just come into your head that you hadn't seen old Steve in rather a long time and you ought to do something about it? Is that how it was?'

'Not exactly.'

'I was afraid it might not be.'

'Though of course there was that too.'

'You don't have to flatter me, you know.'

'It's not flattery. I've thought of you quite a lot, off and on.'

'Only off and on? Now you disappoint me.'

'Well, you wouldn't expect to be in my mind all the time, would you? There are other things.'

He grinned. 'That's so. And now if you want the truth, you've been in my mind too. Off and on.'

'So we're quits on that.'

'Maybe. But you still haven't told me the other reason for your wanting to get in touch with me.'

'That's true.' She hesitated a moment or two, and then, as if deciding to take the plunge, said: 'How would you like to accompany me on a trip to South America?'

His immediate thought was that she was inviting him to take part in another of those dodgy jobs which had landed him in so much trouble in days gone by. And his nerves started vibrating the way they had always done when she had suggested something of the sort. But then he remembered that she was no longer employed by the Intelligence lot, so it had to be a different sort of job – or maybe even no job at all. Though he found it hard to believe that she had sought him out simply because she wanted him to share a holiday jaunt with her down Argentina way, or wherever.

So he said warily, playing for time: 'You're thinking of taking a holiday down there? A package tour for two, maybe?'

'Now don't be stupid,' she said. 'Or pretend to be. You don't really imagine I'm going there for a spot of relaxation in the sun. It's a job, of course.'

'For this Adsum lot? Is that it?'

'Well, who else would it be for?'

'But you haven't yet told me exactly what their line of business is.'

'You don't need to know that. Not immediately, anyway.'

'Hush-hush, is it?'

She just gave a shrug.

He was not sure he liked the sound of this. It smacked rather of the past, when vital information was always being kept from him, so that he was forever working in the dark and stumbling blindly into trouble.

'Am I to take it that you want me to go along with you as an assistant in whatever it is you're intending to do down in that part of the world?'

'That's about it.'

'Why?'

'Well,' she said, 'the fact is my Spanish is not so hot, and as you speak it so well I thought it would be a great help to have you with me.'

'Do your employers know about this?'

'Oh yes.'

'And they approve?'

'They were a bit doubtful at first. But I told them how you'd worked for the Department in the past, and how reliable you'd always been and so on.'

'That was laying it on a bit thick, wasn't it?'

'Possibly. But since I was trying to sell you to them it would hardly have been good policy to dwell on the weaknesses in your character, would it?'

'Weaknesses! What weaknesses?'

'Oh, let's not go into that,' she said.

He let it pass. 'Supposing,' he said, 'you had not been able to find me, or I'd not been available. What then?'

'I'd have had to find somebody else, wouldn't I? But why go into the hypothetical? I have found you and you appear to be available. So how about it?'

'Um—'

'You'll be paid, of course. I imagine you could use the money.'

He reflected that this was no great feat of imagination. He was out of a job, and if he failed to come up with the rent he could be out of the flat as well.

'How much?'

'Oh, four figures at least.'

'And expenses?'

'Now don't overreach yourself.'

'I'll think about it,' Brady said. But he already knew what the answer would be, and he guessed that she knew it too. As on those various occasions in the past, she had him hooked. Not for a moment did he believe that this proposed trip down to some part of South America, as yet unspecified, would turn out to be a simple, straightforward business operation. There would be complications; it was not in the nature of such things that there would not be. And there might even be danger. Oh, most certainly there might.

'Don't look so worried, Steve,' she said. 'There's no risk involved. None at all.'

That was when he knew he would be sticking his neck out again if he went through with this. Because he had heard that line before; and it had never been true, never. So why should it be true in this case either?

Because she was not working for the boys in Whitehall; that was why. She had said goodbye to all that, hadn't she? She had told him so. But might not this new job be of a similar kind? Might not that be why they had taken her on? Because of her experience in undercover work? It seemed possible; even likely.

She might have been reading his thoughts and sensing his reluctance to commit himself, for she said coaxingly: 'I've been counting on you, Steve darling, I really have. You aren't going to let me down, are you? I need you. You do see that, don't you?'

He had never been able to resist when she used that tone of voice with him and looked so appealingly at him. And he could not do it now.

'You really mean that?'

'How can you doubt it?' she said. 'Haven't I always been honest with you?'

He cast his mind back over the years, and he was not so sure about that. Had there not been occasions when she had rather led him by the nose? But had he not always been all too willing to be led when it was she who was doing the leading? So here she was, playing the same old trick on him. He could see her doing it and was not deceived. So maybe this time he would say: 'Nothing doing, Linda darling. It just won't work this time. I've learnt my lesson and you're not catching me again, sweetheart. I'm older and wiser, and you don't catch old birds with chaff.'

She was still watching him closely, and after a few moments she said: 'I think you've made up your mind. You've thought about it and you've come to a decision.'

'Yes,' Brady said, 'I have.'

'And?'

'OK. I'll do it.'

'Ah!' she said. 'I knew you would.'

Chapter Three

INTERVIEW

She said she would have to take him along to see her people, which was the term she used for her employers. Brady gathered that this would be in the nature of a vetting interview, when he would be given the once-over to determine whether he appeared suitable for the job in hand.

'Just a formality,' Linda assured him. 'You couldn't expect them to take you on without even having a look at you.'

'Supposing they don't like what they see?'

'Don't be ridiculous,' she said. 'How could they not?'

Brady thought this might be quite easy for them. But he did not say so. She would have thought he was being defeatist.

'Just smarten yourself up and try to look intelligent.'

'I'll do my best,' he promised. 'I'd hate to let you down.'

He discovered that Adsum Worldwide hung out in a tower block in Docklands. It was a fairly new development and might have appeared large if it had not been dwarfed by the Canada Tower. They travelled down on the Docklands Light Railway, which was a new experience for him, and one that he found quite enjoyable.

'Seems hard to realize,' he said, 'that London used to be a great port and ships in their thousands came up here to discharge their cargoes. Now the work is all done down at Tilbury. Container ships, that sort of thing. Sad, in a way.'

'Now you're being sentimental,' Linda said. 'I don't think it's sad at all. It's progress.'

'And you're all in favour of progress?'

'Of course. You wouldn't want to go back to Dickensian times, would you? When dead bodies were regularly fished out of the Thames.'

'They're still fished out. Though nowadays they're mostly suicides. People jump off the bridges, you know.'

She answered nothing to that; and a few minutes later they were at their destination.

They rode up in a lift to the fifth floor and stepped out into a wide corridor.

'This way,' Linda said. And she set off to the left.

It was not far, and it was not terribly impressive when they reached it. Brady was certainly less than overwhelmed; he had been expecting something rather grander; an extensive array of desks perhaps, complete with all the latest electronic equipment, and a full complement of young men and women beavering away at them. But all there was in the outer office was a bored-looking blonde sitting at the reception desk and paring her fingernails. She obviously knew Linda and had been expecting her.

'Ah, there you are, Miss Manning,' she said. 'It'll be Mr

Lessing 'cause Mr Forder's not in at the moment. This is Mr Braden, is it?'

'Brady,' Linda said. 'Not Braden.'

'Oops!' the blonde said. 'Silly me. Sorry, Mr Brady.'

'Don't let it bother you,' Brady said. 'What's in a name?'

'I'll just see if he's ready for you,' the blonde said.

She called through on an intercom, and it appeared that he was. So she conducted them to the door of an inner office, tapped on it, and announced: 'Miss Manning and Mr Brady, sir.'

They went in and she closed the door on them.

Mr Lessing was built somewhat along the lines of the Michelin Man; he had rather short legs and was globular in the middle, while his head was globular on a smaller scale. He wore rimless glasses, and the eyes behind the lenses were globules of even lesser size. They had the shiny, moist appearance of boiled sweets that had been well sucked. The crown of his head was like a field where the crop had failed, possibly because of drought; what was left of it was patchy and undernourished. His age might have been about forty.

He did not appear to be very busy; he was standing behind a large desk when they went in, with an expanse of window glass at his back. At a guess Brady would have said he had been gazing out of this window, which provided a pleasant view of the river, when the arrival of his two visitors had demanded his attention.

He nodded to Linda and then switched his attention to her companion. 'So, you are Mr Brady.'

Brady affirmed that he was.

'And you wish to work for Adsum Worldwide?'

'That was rather the idea,' Brady said. He felt it unnecessary to add that the originator of the idea was Miss Manning. Lessing probably knew that.

'What do you know of us?'

Brady had to admit that his knowledge of Adsum Worldwide was very limited.

'What has Miss Manning told you?'

'Only that she is being sent on a mission to South America and is in need of an interpreter to help her with the language.'

'And you speak fluent Spanish?'

'Oh yes.'

'I understand you did a job for Whitehall down that way some years ago.'

'Actually it was Central America. Same continent.'

It had been a particularly dirty underhand job, even as such operations went. He was not happy to be reminded of it.

'And other jobs in Europe. Behind the Iron Curtain, as it used the be called.'

'Yes.'

'But you were never officially a government agent. Is that so?'

'Yes. I was pulled in now and then to stick my neck out for the good of my country when they were reluctant to risk anyone more valuable.'

Mr Lessing smiled faintly. 'Do I detect a certain feeling of resentment, Mr Brady?'

Brady shrugged. 'Where would be the point? It's all water under the bridge now. I'm still alive, with just a scar or two to remind me of those days.'

'And also Miss Manning, perhaps?' Lessing cocked an eyebrow.

Brady stared at him coldly. Linda was saying nothing. Her face was expressionless.

He said: 'Until yesterday I had not seen Miss Manning for a long time. We had lost touch with each other.'

'Of course,' Lessing said. 'Of course. Anyway, I can assure you that there will be nothing to fear on this assignment. You will be in no danger at all, so you can put that clean out of your mind.'

Brady abstained from telling him that he had heard this kind of assurance too many times before to take it at face value. He had never put much reliance on it then, and he had usually been proved right not to do so. Therefore, when Lessing offered this assurance it gave him the same uneasy feeling he had experienced when Linda had told him not to look so worried, since there would be no risk involved if he accepted the job. Because when people were at pains to convince you that a certain piece of employment they were offering was as safe as houses it had to mean they thought you would suspect that it was not. And the reason they thought this was simply because you were dead right in your suspicions and the whole thing was as dodgy as a secondhand car dealer.

Well, it was not too late to pull out even now. He had not yet committed himself to anything. He could just say he had changed his mind and walk away. He could, but he knew he would not. For what did he have to go back to? No job and no girlfriend and no flat if he failed to come up with the rent. Not much of a prospect. Weigh that against the assured company of Linda Manning for a time at least, plus some ready money, and it was no contest. He had to go through with the business, come what might. And maybe both Linda and this man Lessing were telling the truth; maybe there was no risk. He did not believe it, but he could be wrong.

'Well now,' Lessing said, 'I don't think there's much else to discuss.'

'You haven't told me yet just what the job is,' Brady said.

'Oh, that's not necessary. Miss Manning will fill you in on the details. Just do as she says. OK?'

He seemed impatient to be rid of them. Perhaps he had work to do, but Brady doubted it. In one corner of the office was a putter and a golf ball, and it seemed more than possible that he had been practising his short game on the carpet before the two visitors arrived. Maybe he was eager to get back to the exercise. Golfers were all nutcases in Brady's opinion. They seemed to become obsessed with the game.

When they were walking away from the building Brady said: 'Am I to take it that I've been approved, would you say?'

'Of course. Like I said, it was just a formality. What did you think of our Mr Lessing?'

'He didn't strike me as being a live wire exactly.'

'You mustn't judge by appearances. He's no fool.'

'I'll take your word for it. What's the other one like?'

'Forder? Oh, he's very different. Skinny little man and sharp as a needle. Something of a workaholic. He's the real brains of the outfit. My reading is that he took Lessing as a partner for financial reasons.'

'You mean it was Lessing who had the capital to get the business running, whatever that business is, and Forder contributed the know-how.'

'Something like that, I imagine. Though I don't know much about it. The company was on the go long before I got taken on.'

'You applied for the job, did you?'

'Yes. I answered an advertisement in a paper, had an interview, and that was that. They seemed to like me.'

'Who wouldn't? And how many other agents do they employ?'

'I've no idea. It's all a bit secretive, you know. They tend to keep things compartmentalized. I never know what any of the others are doing. They could be operating anywhere – in this country or abroad.'

'So you don't have any contact with them?'

'As a rule, no.'

'So now are you going to tell me what kind of business it is?'

'Oh,' she said, 'let's not go into all that right now. As soon as you need to know I'll put you in the picture.'

He had to leave it at that. He wondered whether it was a habit she had retained from the old days. Always keeping him in the dark. No need for him to know everything. He was just there to carry out orders and not ask too many questions.

'I suppose your passport is in order?'

'Yes. And it's genuine. Not like some of those I had in the past, with false names on them.'

'Good. You'll need a visa for Paraguay, but there should be no trouble over that.'

'Paraguay! So that's where we're going?'

'Yes. Didn't I tell you?'

'You know you didn't. It was just somewhere in South America. I was hoping it might be Brazil. Copacabana Beach and all that jazz. I don't think Paraguay has much to offer in that line.'

'I don't suppose it does. But this isn't a pleasure trip we're going on, you know. It's business.'

'I suppose so.'

It was when they were travelling back in a carriage on the Docklands Light Railway that Brady made a suggestion.

'Lock,' he said, 'it's been a long time since we were last

teamed up. So why don't we do a bit of celebrating?'

She gave him a quizzical glance. 'You think our getting together again is a good reason for celebrating?'

'For my money it's the best of reasons.'

She appeared to be giving some serious thought to the suggestion. Then she said: 'I suppose there wouldn't be any harm in it.'

It was hardly the most enthusiastic of acceptances, but he had not expected her to utter a cry of joy at the prospect; it would not have been in her nature. He was happy enough that she had not dismissed the suggestion out of hand.

'What precisely,' she asked, 'did you have in mind?'

'Oh, I thought we might go somewhere for a meal as a start. After which I'm sure we could think of something. The evening lies ahead and the night is ours.'

'Now, now,' she said. 'Don't get carried away. One thing at a time. Remember that this is strictly a business relationship. You do understand that?'

'Yes, of course.'

Which was what it had always been in the past. But somehow the borderline between business and pleasure had had a tendency to become blurred and even to vanish completely. And maybe something of the sort might happen again. Maybe an evening on the town would lead to more intimate activities – at his place or even at hers.

Maybe.

Chapter Four

DOGSBODY

In the event it turned out to be hers. And this, in a way, was an indication that things had changed; for in all the time he had known her and operated with her in the past she had never taken him to her pad; had never revealed the address of it to him. In those days it had always been she who got in touch with him; never the other way round. He had accepted the arrangement and had concluded that for someone in the undercover game it was advisable not to reveal to all and sundry just where she lived. Her name had not even been in the telephone directory.

Now apparently, with the change of employment, had come a relaxation of the need for secrecy, and he was at last permitted to visit the place which she called home. Though it was likely of course that, like him, she had moved from the former abode and was now living in different quarters. Whether this was so or not, he could see at a glance that her place was a step or two higher in the estate agents' pecking order than his.

It was a maisonette in a quiet side-street not far from the Bayswater Road, in first-class condition and certainly worth quite a pot of money at today's prices. He wondered whether she owned it or whether it was rented, but she did not volunteer the information and he hesitated to ask.

'This is nice,' he said, when they were inside. 'This is very nice indeed.'

And it was. It was furnished in style; which was no more than he would have expected of her. She had good taste, that was apparent; but he could detect no male influence anywhere, so it seemed that the Mr Potts to whom she had once been married had failed to leave his mark on this nest he had shared with her. Or maybe she had erased any indication of his former presence as thoroughly as she had erased his surname from her signature.

'You like it, then?'

'Very much. It's so absolutely you, if you see what I mean. It's chic.'

He could see that she was pleased. And then she said: 'I haven't been here long. When I was married to Herbert I left my old place and went to live with him. He's got this house in Hampstead. It's big; been in the family for generations. I never liked it; too gloomy. Full of old oak furniture, practically black, heavy as lead. Wallpaper that looked as if it been there in Victorian times; oil paintings so grimy you could hardly tell whether they were landscapes or interiors; no feeling of joy anywhere.'

'Well,' Brady said, 'you must have known what you were taking on when you married him. So why did you do it?'

'A stroke of midsummer madness, I suppose. He had a certain charm about him, and a persuasive way of talking. Maybe I just let him talk me into it when I was feeling a bit down. Later I realized just how incompatible we were.'

'What was he doing for a living?'

'He was in the City. Still is, I suppose. Wheeling and dealing. Just making money out of nothing. Never really producing anything useful. You know the way it is. It's people like him who make London tick.'

'How about you? Did you give up the old job?'

She shook her head. 'Not as long as there was one. He didn't like that. He complained that he never knew where I was, when I'd be at home. I suppose he had a point; he wanted to start a family and he had these old-fashioned ideas about a wife's place being at the hearthside, bringing up children, entertaining guests, seeing to the housekeeping, that sort of thing. For me it simply wasn't on. You do see, don't you?'

He saw very clearly. He simply could not picture her in that sort of life; looking after the home while this Potts character was away in the City coining money. What would she have done with her spare time? Join women's groups, potter around in the garden, paint, watch television? It would all have seemed so tame after what had gone before. Without ever having seen Herbert Potts, he had a mental picture of the man: a stick, fussy, starchy, narrow-minded, domineering. How could she ever have imagined that marriage to someone like that would be a success? It must have been doomed to failure from the start.

And of course he was glad it had failed. He would not have wanted her to be stuck in that gloomy old Hampstead house with the deplorable Potts, giving birth to a brood of little Pottses and living under the disapproving eyes of Potts's forebears as they gazed down from those grimy oil paintings in their tarnished gilt frames that hung on the interior walls of that ancestral home.

He realized that this mental picture of the Potts ménage was in all probability an utterly false one, but it mattered not. What was quite certain was that the man had never been the right husband for Linda, and apparently she herself had soon realized it. A case of marry in haste and repent at leisure, no doubt.

The kitchen at the maisonette had everything. It was the kind you saw in the housekeeping magazines and the colour supplements; the kind in which hopeful salesmen, and even saleswomen, were forever trying to get you interested by ringing you up at inconvenient moments in the evening or lunch hour. It gleamed with stainless steel and cream enamel. There was a gas cooker, looking brand new, a microwave, a twin sink unit, a fridge-freezer and an automatic washing-machine and a dishwasher. There were racks of cook's knives and tiers of pots and pans, and rows of cupboards with cedarwood doors.

'You throw many parties?' Brady asked.

'No. Scarcely any. I'm not a party person.'

'With all this going to waste?'

'I wouldn't call it waste,' she said. 'And I do have the odd visitor.'

'Is that what I am? An odd visitor.'

'The oddest, Steve. I can't think of anyone odder.'

'Now you're kidding,' he said. But he could not be sure of it and he let it go.

The bathroom was quite a showpiece too. The bath was one of those which two people could share with no fear of overcrowding. And later that evening two people did just that.

Brady was delighted to observe that Linda still had the kind of body that, unrobed, was a treat to look at: slender, with firm breasts which gave no hint of sagging, trim waist and dancer's legs. He wondered just how much effort and maybe hard cash it took to keep the ravages of time at bay and achieve this desirable result. Or did it for her just come naturally?

'You're lovely,' he said. 'You're just as lovely as ever you were. And that's really saying something. How do you manage it?'

She answered with a laugh: 'Will power. And if it comes to that, you haven't worn so badly yourself. So how do you do it?'

'I've no idea. I guess it's just the way I was made. Good durable material.'

'No regular sessions in a gym, pumping iron, that sort of thing?'

'What me! You have to be joking. That's hard work, you know. And it costs a lot, so I've been told. Did Potts do anything in that line?'

'He surely did. It was an obsession with him. Weighed himself every day to check that he wasn't putting on the pounds, or should we say the kilos? A few ounces over the mark was a major disaster.'

'Sounds like a neurotic.'

'Maybe he was. Maybe he still is.'

'Do you ever see him?'

'Very seldom. Practically never in fact. He's married again.'

'What's the new one like?'

'A fluffy blonde. Much younger than him. Not remarkable for intelligence, I'd say.'

Brady grinned. 'From one extreme to the other, eh? You're not peeved, are you?'

'Me? Of course not. Why should I be? Obviously he wanted a change and I suppose he's happy with the swap.' Then, switching the subject, she said: 'I see you've still got it.'

'Got what?'

'The scar.'

'Oh that. Well, I'm hardly likely to lose it, am I? It's a fixture, a permanent blemish and an ever-present reminder of what I did for Queen and Country long ago.'

'Not so very long.'

'Maybe not. But it seems like it.'

'Anyway, it doesn't spoil your looks. Not down there. I imagine very few people get to see it.'

'Just people I bath with.'

It was quite a small scar, slightly below the ribs on the left hand side. That was where the East German doctor had inserted while he was unconscious the piece of metal plating which he, all unwittingly, had carried across from one side of the Iron Curtain to the other. And she, Linda, had been waiting for him, with some others; waiting for him to get home and dry. God, had he been glad to see her!

So then they had taken the metal out of him and sewn him up again, leaving the scar to remind him.

'Was it really worth all the trouble?'

'Oh,' she said, 'I expect so. Every little piece of information we picked up from the Communist bloc helped us to keep ahead in the arms race.'

'So you don't think I risked my life and shed my blood and languished for a time in durance vile to no purpose?'

'Never believe it. Whatever gave you that idea?'

'It was just a thought. It would probably all have turned out just the way it did even if I had never done a thing.'

'If it comes to the point,' she said, 'we could all have thoughts like that. It just doesn't do to dwell on them; it's too depressing. You did some good work, Steve, and it helped. Besides, it wasn't all bad, was it?'

'That's true. There were interludes. I remember a sauna by a lake in Finland. Just you and me. But it didn't last. Nothing good lasts. That's the pity of it.'

He tried to think when he had last made love to her. Had it been on that holiday in Jamaica when he had briefly been in funds? Maybe.

He said: 'I can't think why we never got married.'

'I did,' she said. 'To Herbert.'

'I meant to each other.'

She gave a laugh. 'I'll tell you why. Because it was just not on. You never had a decent job. You were living from hand to mouth in that squalid little dump you called a flat. I'd have had to support you, Steve, and I was just not prepared to do that.'

He had to admit that there some truth in what she had said.

'Besides which,' she said, 'as I recall, you never asked me.'

'There was that too,' he said. And he wondered whether the situation had effectively changed much now. He was again out of a regular job; and though his flat was not quite such a dump as the old place had been, it looked as though he might soon lose possession of it if he did not find other remunerative employment pretty soon. There was of course the money he was hoping to get in payment for this South American venture, whatever it might be; but this would not last for long, and after that he could see nothing in prospect. Proposals of marriage, therefore, appeared to be well and truly out of the question. Which was a pity really, because the more he saw of the lovely Linda Manning, the more attractive a future with her forever by his side appeared to be.

He noticed that she was gazing at him in what he could only describe in his mind as a speculative sort of way, as though she for her part might be considering the pros and cons of another entry into the matrimonial business. But when she spoke it was not on that subject at all.

'What,' she asked, 'do you know about Paraguay?'

'To be perfectly honest,' he said, 'not a lot. I seem to remember that the country had a president of German descent who was a bit of a bad egg and finally got kicked out. I forget his name.'

'Stroessner. General Alfredo Stroessner. I understand the country has progressed quite a lot since they got rid of him. It's more democratic.'

'I'm glad to hear it. I'm not terribly keen on dictators. Anyway, I don't suppose I have to be an expert on Paraguayan history to do this job.'

'Not really, no.'

'So all I have to do is act as interpreter. Is that it?'

'That's about it.'

'And help with the luggage and and all that sort of thing.'

'Naturally.'

'A kind of general dogsbody in fact.'

'Exactly. Do you think you can manage it?'

'I'll do my best.'

'OK,' she said. 'We'll settle for that.'

Chapter Five

NO GUN

Brady had never enjoyed air travel. To him it seemed much like a long train journey in a crowded carriage without the scenery: dead boring in fact. This latest flight was made less boring than usual only by the fact that Linda Manning was occupying the seat next to his.

'How much more civilized a journey like this would have been in the old days,' he said. 'Imagine it: the long sea voyage, day after day with nothing to do but relax in deckchairs and watch the dolphins and flying-fish or stretch your legs on the promenade deck. And finally all the excitement of coming into port in a strange land.'

'You couldn't have done it,' she said.

'What do you mean, couldn't have done it?'

'Paraguay is landlocked. It has no seaport.'

'Now you're splitting hairs,' he said. And then after a while: 'Have you still got that gun in your handbag like you used to have?'

'Don't be stupid,' she said. 'You know they check you for things like that before you're allowed to board a plane.'

'Hijackers still seem to manage to smuggle them aboard.'

'Well, we're not hijackers. And besides, why would I need a gun? Paraguay is a republic now. It's civilized.'

'And law-abiding?'

'I see no reason to suppose not. South American countries are not as anarchic as they used to be. Times have changed. The people are more peaceable.'

'As in Colombia, for instance?'

'Colombia is a special case. It's the cocaine racket that spoils things there. Too many people getting rich by trading in the drug and having their own private armies which the government can't bring under control. Fortunately, the coca shrub doesn't grow in Paraguay.'

'I'm glad to hear it,' Brady said.

At least he could rest assured that whatever business it was that was taking Linda to Paraguay had nothing to do with drug barons or cartels. And that was a comforting thought.

The last part of the flight was made in an aging twin-engined Boeing, the passengers in which presented a mixture of the various racial types which made up the population of that part of the world: Spanish, Indian, German, with even a few Orientals: Japanese, Chinese and Koreans, to add spice to the human brew. On what kind of business all these individuals were travelling to Asunción Brady could not guess, but he had no desire to find out. It would be sufficient for him to discover why he and Linda were going to that part of the world, which as far as he knew had little enough to attract the casual visitor.

It had to be business, of course. The capital of a country as large as Paraguay, even if this were not one of the richest of them, must be of some importance as a centre of trade and industry.

And in fact it was even a port of sorts, since it was situated on the Paraguay River near its confluence with the Pilcomayo flowing down from the foothills of the Andes. Downstream these two would become the Parana, making a liquid highway to Buenos Aires and the great estuary of the Rio de la Plata. There was a railway too, snaking down through Argentina, that rich neighbour to the south, but Brady did not anticipate that he and Linda would do any travelling by river or rail. though of course there could be no certainty of that. Anything might happen, and he could only wait and see what the future would bring forth. All would no doubt be eventually revealed.

His first impression of Asunción when they had left the airport was not of a city that might have been described as a jewel of the southern hemisphere; but he had not expected that it would be, and he was not disappointed. And though it was no rival to Rio de Janeiro or Buenos Aires or even Montevideo, it was, he supposed, good enough in its way. The Spanish had settled there centuries ago, making of it a centre for their colonization of the southern part of the continent, and they had left their mark. In some ways it might have been an old town in Spain, with the inevitable slums where the poor led their deprived existence.

The hotel which he and Linda made their immediate base was modest in style, but she maintained that it would suit them admirably.

'We don't want to be ostentatious, now do we?'

'Perish the thought,' Brady said. Though he did wonder what would have been ostentatious in going to a rather less depressing establishment than this. There was a kind of shabby genteel look about it, as though it had begun life in rather better circumstances but had gradually come down in the world. 'I wonder whether stout Cortés ever slept here.'

'Cortés was never in these parts,' she said, rather tartly. 'So don't try to be smart.'

There was a woman at the reception desk; middle-aged, stout, with straight black hair, rather greasy in appearance, and features that might have been carved from mahogany. Not once during their exchanges with her did the faintest flicker of a smile soften her sombre features. It was presumably not in her contract to be charming to prospective guests.

Brady did the talking; it was what he had been engaged to do and he intended to earn his pay. And then a bellhop who looked as if he had grown old and rickety in sympathy with the hotel conducted them to their room on the second floor.

It was about what might have been expected: a trifle shabby, a trifle worn and faded, bearing the evidence of a host of previous occupants; the furniture showing the marks of those transients who, over the course of years, had come and gone; whence and whither, who could say? Hotel rooms, good or bad, were like that, Brady mused; haunted by the spirits of former guests.

'Well,' Linda said, 'what do you think of it?'

'Hardly home sweet home, is it?'

'What do you expect? You travel four or five thousand miles and hope to find a replica of that place you occupy in London? Such as it is.'

She sounded rather peeved, as though any criticism of the hotel accommodation constituted a reflection on her judgement, since she had chosen it.

Brady hastened to placate her. 'No. It's fine. I've known worse. Oh yes, a lot worse. Thus is a palace compared to some of the dumps I've kipped in.'

'I can well believe that. And at least there's a bathroom.'

Which was true. Even if there were rust streaks on the bath and a hammering noise came from the pipes when any of the taps were turned on. An odour of disinfectant fought with and overpowered any other scent that might have lingered there.

'Anyway,' Linda said, as though to nip in the bud any criticism of the sanitary facilities, 'we shall not be staying here for long.'

'So you're proposing to move on?'

'It will be necessary, I imagine.'

'I'll take your word for that. So what's the next move?'

It was still afternoon, and he did not suppose she intended hanging around in a dingy hotel room waiting for something to turn up. Her answer corroborated this.

'Our next move is we go and see a man.'

'About a dog?'

She answered rather sharply. 'Don't be facetious. This is serious business.'

'I never doubted it,' Brady said. 'The man has a name?'

'Naturally. It's Pedro Ruiz.'

'And this Señor Ruiz is expecting us?'

'He's expecting someone. Not necessarily us.'

'Better not keep him waiting then. You have the address?'

'Yes.'

'So let's be on our way.'

Chapter Six

RUIZ

They took a taxi, which the unsmiling receptionist ordered for them. Brady thought the driver looked surprised when Linda gave him the address, but he made no comment. He was a swarthy character with a black moustache of luxuriant growth, a beak of a nose and prominent cheekbones. He was wearing an oil-smeared baseball cap, and he would not have appeared out of place in a band of brigands. Possibly cab-driving was a spare-time job; a sideline.

It was quite a long ride, and it soon became apparent that they were being taken to one of the less salubrious parts of the town, where buildings were old and run down and there was a lot of garbage lying around with skinny dogs and swarms of flies feeding on it. Here there were no supermarkets, no smart boutiques or glittering jewellers' windows to attract the moneyed clientele. Indeed, it was doubtful whether any of the moneyed clientele ever ventured into this area; they would have been afraid of being mugged.

'I don't care much for the look of this,' Brady said. 'This seems like a pretty rough district.'

'You worry too much,' Linda said.

'Well, you know me. It's my nature.'

He wondered whether she was worried too. If she was, she gave no indication of it. So perhaps this was what she had expected and had not felt it necessary to warn him in advance. Just like the old days.

The driver took a side turning into an even meaner mean street and drove more slowly. In one place a gang of urchins was playing amid the rubble of a building that had either been knocked down or had collapsed under the influence of age and decay. Further along a dented and rusting car was standing by the gutter on wood blocks, the wheels having been removed and carried away. Men, apparently with nothing better to do, were lounging in doorways, clotting here and there into little groups. Slatternly women formed other groups or went about their business with baskets on their arms, while more mangy dogs lay in the sun and scratched themselves for fleas.

The cab slowed even more as the driver scanned the buildings on each side, apparently searching for the address. Finally he brought the vehicle to a halt by the kerb and indicated that they had reached their destination.

'So this is it,' Brady said. 'Nice.'

It was a house that matched other buildings in that quarter: stucco walls from which slabs of the plaster were falling away; three storeys; rusty iron balconies under the first-floor windows; some washing hanging out here and there . . .

They got out, the driver remaining in his seat.

'Tell him,' Linda said, 'to wait here for us.'

Brady passed the message on, and it did not go down very well with the man behind the black moustache. He seemed to have a desire to be on his way and not have to stay for an indefinite period stationary in that place. Possibly he had taken note of the car with no wheels and felt that his taxi might end up in a similar condition if he hung around too long. He suggested with some emphasis that he would like to be paid at once for the journey he had already made.

Brady started to give the English version of this demand to Miss Manning, but she appeared to have got the gist of it anyway.

'You can tell him,' she said, 'he'll get his money when he's taken us back to our hotel and not before.'

As he was translating this, Brady could see that the cabbie was not taking it at all well. In fact he looked pretty angry, and Brady had an uneasy feeling that he might suddenly pull out a gun and threaten to start shooting if he did not get his money pronto.

But Linda had already turned away, and Brady followed suit, while the cabbie expressed his disgruntlement by muttering imprecations which were fortunately untranslatable.

There was a door standing open at the front of the building, and Linda walked inside with Brady at her heels. They found themselves in a kind of lobby with a narrow staircase leading up from it and a passageway on one side. It was pretty gloomy, most of what light there was coming in from the doorway. There was an odour of decay and ancient cooking and much else besides, none of it pleasant.

'Are you sure this is where your man hangs out?' Brady asked. 'It doesn't look the sort of place anyone would want to be seen dead in.'

She answered rather acidly: 'Most people would prefer not to be seen dead in any sort of place. They'd rather stay alive.'

'Well, you know what I mean.'

'Yes, I do know. And whatever you may think probable or improbable, my information is that this is where our man does hang out. When he's at home, that is.'

'So you think he could be out?'

'Anything's possible.'

A woman appeared out of the shadow further down the passageway and came towards them. There was a blowzy look about her; she was wearing a loose cotton dress with no sleeves and a pair of dirty white trainers on her feet. She had a shuffling walk, and her heavy breathing was audible as she approached.

'Ask her,' Linda said, 'whether Ruiz lives here.'

The woman had come to a halt. They were standing between her and the doorway and she was too broad in the beam to have gone past without elbowing one or the other aside. She was staring at them in no very friendly fashion but saying nothing.

Brady put the question to her, but she made no immediate reply; she looked wary as well as somewhat hostile. Possibly she was naturally suspicious of all strangers, especially two who appeared so out of place in those surroundings.

Then, as if with some reluctance, she said: 'Why do you want to know?'

'We wish to talk to him.'

'And suppose he has no wish to talk to you?'

'There is no reason why he should not. It could be to his advantage. And he is expecting us.'

This argument seemed to do the trick. The woman glanced from him to Linda and back again. Then she jerked a thumb in the direction of the stairs and said: 'Next floor. Number five.'

Brady thanked her and moved aside to give her room to pass. But she did not immediately leave the building; she stood and watched them as they climbed the bare, creaking stairs, as if to make sure they were on the right track.

They reached a landing, as bare of covering as the stairs. There was a passageway, dimly lighted by a window at the far end, and a short way along it they came to a door with the number five marked on it in white paint.

'This seems to be what we're looking for,' Brady said. 'You want me to knock?'

'Go ahead.'

He gave a rap on the door with his knuckles, and they waited. There was no response.

'Maybe he's not at home,' Brady said.

'Or maybe he's just playing hard to get. Try again.'

This time he rapped so vigorously it hurt his knuckles. But the self-inflicted pain had its reward: they heard someone shuffling across the floor of the room, and then a croaking voice demanded to be told who was there.

'Señor Ruiz?' Brady inquired.

'That's me. What you want?'

'A word or two. Business.'

'What sort of business?'

'Important. What you've been expecting. We're from England.'

It was this last part that seemed to reassure the unseen occupant of number five. They could hear a key grating in the lock. The knob turned and the door was pulled open a few inches to allow a pair of eyes to peer out. Brady felt that he had never seen a more cadaverous face than that in which the eyes were set. It looked as though the owner might have been at death's door rather than at the door of a wretched room on the first floor of a decaying old building. The cheeks were hollow, bones standing out like crags, lips bluish in colour, grey stubble overall.

'You'd better let us in,' Brady said. 'We've come a long way to see you, and we're not going to make much progress standing out here, you know.'

The logic of this appeared to get through to the man. He stepped back and pulled the door further open. Linda went in first and Brady followed. Ruiz thrust his head and scrawny neck outside to glance up and down the passageway, as if to make sure no one else was out there, and then closed and locked the door. He appeared very nervous and his movements were erratic. He seemed unable to control a shaking in all his limbs, though he was obviously making an effort to do so.

The room was a mess and the floor was just bare boards. There was a camp-bed pushed up close to the wall opposite the door. On it a coarse grey blanket and some dirty bed-linen looked as though they had not been touched since their owner had crawled out of them in the morning, or whatever time of the day it had been. The place stank; it was rancid; there was filth everywhere. Brady had a feeling that if he touched anything he would be contaminated.

Besides the bed there were only a few sticks of furniture: a sagging, worn-out armchair, springs showing like a kind of mushroom growth; one or two other chairs, rickety as invalids, with piles of junk on them; an old bureau, open, papers in disordered heaps, and in amongst the papers a hypodermic syringe that looked as septic as a festering wound.

Ruiz was wearing a filthy singlet and a pair of ragged cotton slacks; his feet were bare and grimy, the toenails long and almost black. He seemed to have no chest to speak of; from the shoulders down to the waist he was concave. Brady noticed the puncture marks in his arms and guessed what the hypodermic had been used for. The man was a junkie, no doubt about it. And he had the shakes. He was probably in need of a fix, and maybe he had run out of the stuff. Maybe he had also run out of the cash needed to buy more.

He made a half-hearted gesture towards the chairs, as if inviting them to sit down, but abandoned it when neither visitor showed any inclination to accept the offer.

'Ask him,' Linda said, 'whether he has something for us.' But then she added immediately: 'No, don't bother. I'll ask him myself.'

And she did so. In Spanish.

Brady was not altogether surprised. He had had a pretty shrewd idea that she was not so ignorant of that language as she would have had him believe. Now he was sure of it. Apparently it had just suited her to play along with the deception for a while, but now the time had come to abandon it. It was much the sort of thing he would have expected of her.

Ruiz answered warily: 'What would you expect me to have?'

'A name. An address.'

'And if I have something of that sort which you want, I would need to be paid for it.'

'Very well. But first answer the question. Do you have it?'

For answer Ruiz went to the bureau, searched in a cubby-hole and extracted from a bundle of other papers a grubby buff envelope, sealed and marked on the outside simply by a small cross. He held it in one clawlike hand and showed it to them.

'What you are looking for is inside.'

'Let us see.'

Ruiz shook his shaggy head. 'Oh no. First we have to agree a price. Then you pay me and then you have the envelope.'

'You're crazy,' she said. 'Do you think we're going to pay you for something we haven't even seen? The envelope could be empty and then where would we be?'

'No, it is not empty. I assure you.'

'Then open it and show us.'

Ruiz gave a cackling laugh. 'Now who's crazy? I show you what is inside. You read it. Then you pay me nothing, because you already have what you came for. In your head.'

'So you don't trust us?'

'Why would I trust you? I never saw you before.'

'He's got a point there,' Brady said.

'Are you saying we should pay him whatever he asks and take a pig in a poke?'

'It's stalemate otherwise.'

She gave a shrug. 'I suppose you're right. We were directed to him by Adsum, so I guess he must be the genuine article even if he doesn't look it.'

She turned again to Ruiz and switched back to Spanish. 'Very well, have it your way. So what is the price?'

Ruiz answered without hesitation: 'Five hundred dollars. American.'

She stared at him. 'Five hundred dollars! You really are out of your mind.'

'It is the price,' Ruiz said.

'Well, it's far too high. Let us say one hundred, and that is being generous.'

Ruiz was unmoved. 'Five hundred it is. You want the envelope, you pay the money. Cash.'

He seemed very firm on this, though the hand holding the envelope was shaking. Maybe, Brady thought, he was in truly dire need of the money to buy more of the junk he was pumping into his arm. Maybe he was clean out of it and desperate to get a fresh supply. Maybe he even owed money to the dealers and they were leaning on him to get it. Something was making him obstinate.

'I don't have that amount on me,' Linda said.

Ruiz shrugged. 'You can get it.'

'Better let him have it.' Brady said. 'After all, what's the odds? It's not your money.'

She appeared to come to the same conclusion. 'Very well, Señor Ruiz, you win. We will get the money for you, but it will not be today. If we come tomorrow morning you will be here?'

He gave a wry grin. 'Where else would I be?'

Chapter Seven

NICE NEIGHBOURHOOD

They went back down the creaking stairs and out of the building into the afternoon sunshine. The taxi was still there, but the driver was having trouble with a gang of urchins. They were taunting him and threatening him with stones. They might already have thrown some at the vehicle, but the situation was a stand-off now, because the man had produced a revolver and was aiming it at them. There was little doubt that he would have been prepared to use it if there had been further provocation, and the kids knew it; they were holding their fire, but they were not going away.

Linda and Brady got into the cab. The driver was swearing and appeared to be in a vile mood. He had to put down the revolver in order to start the engine and get the vehicle moving. He drove down the street for a little way and made a U-turn and came back. The kids were standing in the middle of the road and he drove straight at them, gaining speed. They had to move fast to avoid being mowed down. The cab went past and had put a fair distance between it and the gang before any of them had recovered sufficiently to hurl a scatter of stones to speed it on its way. Only one or two found their target, and no glass was broken.

'Nice kids,' Brady said. 'Nice neighbourhood.'

'You have to take the rough with the smooth,' Linda said.

'I didn't see any smooth back there. All looked pretty rough to me.'

The driver was saying nothing, but the back of his neck seemed to speak for him, and it was easy to tell that he was really burned up about the way things had gone.

'Something warns me,' Brady said, 'that we'll not get this boy to take us down here again.'

'Then we shall just have to find somebody else, won't we?'

It seemed to Brady that his companion was taking everything very calmly. He, for his part, was not looking forward with any pleasure to paying another visit to that part of town. There was an impression of lawlessness, even of menace, about it. Quite apart from those damned kids. But one thing was certain: Linda was not going to be put off paying another call on Pedro Ruiz; and she would expect him to accompany her, even though she had now made it plain that she had no need of his services in the interpreting line. And that was another thing.

'You've been having me on, haven't you?'

She gave him a glance of complete innocence. 'Having you on, Steve? In what way?'

'You can speak Spanish as well as I can.'

'Actually, no,' she said. 'That's not strictly true. Not quite as well. After all, you were brought up to it when you were in Spain as a child. Isn't that so?'

'Maybe. But you speak it well enough to get by without my help. Why did you pretend you couldn't?'

'I had to have some excuse for roping you in, didn't I?'

'You must have wanted me very badly.'

'Now,' she said, 'don't let it go to your head. I've no doubt I could have found somebody else without too much trouble.'

But he was not taken in by this. She had wanted him. Otherwise, why would she have gone to bother of running him to earth? She must have wanted him more than a little.

He liked that.

Then he said: 'We could have taken that envelope, you know. Ruiz wouldn't have been able to prevent us. It would have been dead easy. He'd have been a pushover.'

'Do you think I don't know that? Of course it would have been easy. But it doesn't happen to be the way I do business.'

'So you have a conscience?'

She ignored that. 'And besides,' she said, 'I doubt whether Adsum would approve of that sort of thing. They may want to do business with him again.'

'I suppose so. But what surprises me is that they should ever think of using a man like that as their agent in this part of the world. He's obviously a drug addict.'

'Maybe he wasn't on the stuff when they started using him. Maybe they have no idea what he's like now. Anyway, I'm not really sure you could call him an agent. More of an occasional go-between.'

'You yourself have had no dealings with him before?'

'Oh, no. This is the first time I've been sent to these parts.'

'But you have travelled to other countries for Adsum?'

'On occasion, yes.'

'How long have you been working for them?'

'Long enough.'

Long enough for what? he wondered. But he did not ask.

*

There was some argument about the fare when they got back to the hotel. The driver demanded a steep increase on what it would normally have been because of the unpleasantness he had been forced to endure. Besides which, there was the damage to his cab inflicted by the stone-throwing urchins to be taken into consideration.

Linda told him scathingly that the cab had been in such a wretched condition from the start that you would have needed the eye of a hawk to see where any new damage had been added.

This aspersion on his vehicle sent the driver into quite a paroxysm of rage. If the sexual morals of his mother had been put in question he could hardly have been more offended. Some of the words he was using were outside Brady's vocabulary, and he intended keeping them there. He doubted whether they would have done much for his standing in polite Spanish society. Always supposing that he should ever find himself in that kind of society. Which seemed doubtful.

'Better give him the money, Linda,' he said. 'Don't want to make a scene and bring the coppers running, do we?'

She seemed quite prepared to do just that, but finally decided to compromise by forking out a sum just halfway between the normal fare and the exorbitant amount that the cabbie was demanding. The man accepted it with a very bad grace, but to Brady's relief made no move to bring out the revolver as a persuader. They watched him drive away and then went into the hotel.

There was a bank not far away, and fairly early in the morning they paid a visit to it. Linda had brought a supply of traveller's cheques and she drew on them for the amount in dollars that Ruiz had demanded.

They found a taxi and gave the address. The driver was rather more prepossessing than the one who had driven them there on the previous day. He was younger and was decently shaved. He made no comment when he heard where they wished to be taken, and showed no surprise.

'You know where that is?' Linda asked.

'I know.'

It did not seem quite so bad when they got there. They could see no street urchins around, so perhaps the gang had turned its attention to other parts. When the cab pulled up at the door of the building the driver made no objection to waiting for them while they carried out whatever business they had to do. Brady hoped he would have no reason to regret this willingness.

They encountered no one in the lobby or on the stairs. Indeed, the whole house seemed oddly quiet, as though it had been completely deserted. When they came to the door of Ruiz's room they discovered that it was not locked; in fact the slight pressure of Brady's knuckles when he rapped on it caused it to swing inward with a faint squeaking of hinges. And then the reason why there had been this lack of resistance became apparent in the splintered timber of the door frame. Someone had obviously forced it open, either by a lever or a violent blow.

Brady did not care for the look of it. The door was still only partly open, and there was no sound coming from inside the room.

'I think,' he said, 'our Mr Ruiz has had visitors. And unwelcome ones at that. Perhaps we should now go back down those stairs and get to hell out of here.'

Linda stared at him. 'Are you mad? We've come here to pick up a piece of important information. Or had you forgotten that small detail?'

'No, I hadn't forgotten. I just have this odd feeling that we may be getting involved in something I for one would much rather not be involved in.'

'Now you're talking nonsense,' she said. 'Come along.' And she pushed the door with her foot and walked into the room.

Brady followed her, and one look was enough to convince him that all his misgivings had been only too well founded.

'Oh dear!' he said. 'Oh dear, oh dear, oh dear!'

The room was in a mess; though perhaps not so very much more of a mess than it had been in the previous day. But now there was a difference, and a very vital one, since,it involved the person who was the lawful occupant of the room, such as it was; the one who had maybe called it home and might even have felt secure in the grubby little retreat from the cares of the world.

But it was all too evident that if he had in fact felt so, he had been living in a fool's paradise. A shoddy lock on an equally shoddy door had been no adequate defence against a criminal intent on breaking in. That outer world, so hopefully intended to be kept at bay by this door and this lock, had brushed aside the weak impediment and come rushing in like a tidal wave breaking through a bank of shingle.

The result was there to see in the body of Pedro Ruiz, stretched out on the floor, face upward and eyes staring at the ceiling as if trying to decipher some cryptic message scrawled on that dirty white surface.

'Oh dear!' Brady said again. 'I don't care for the look of this at all.'

'Nobody's asking you to like it,' Miss Manning said tartly. 'But that's neither here nor there.' And she pushed the door shut, again using her foot.

Brady was of the opinion that it was very much here, even if it was not there. And he said so.

'My God!' Linda said. 'One would think you'd never seen a dead body before. And you have, haven't you?'

Brady had to admit that he had – as she very well knew, since she had on more than one occasion been with him at the time. 'But I never cared much for them, you know. They tend to give me the creeps. Maybe I'm just allergic to this sort of thing.'

Pedro Ruiz in death looked even less attractive than he had done in life. He had been stabbed several times: in the chest, in the abdomen and in the throat; which seemed a shade excessive and might have been indicative of frenzy on the part of the attacker. Any one of the wounds would have been sufficient to snuff out the life of the man on the floor. He had bled freely, and probably quite recently, judging by the colour of the blood, which contrasted starkly with the ghastly pallor of the victim's face. The knife that had been used was nowhere to be seen, so presumably the killer had taken it away with him.

'Don't touch anything,' Linda said. 'We don't want to leave any fingerprints.'

Brady had had no intention of touching anything, especially the corpse. And his inclination was to get out of that damned room in double-quick time. But Linda seemed to be in no hurry to depart.

It looked as though whoever had killed Ruiz had made a

thorough search of the room, concentrating especially on the bureau. This had obviously been ransacked; drawers pulled out, contents spilled on the floor, nothing replaced.

'I wonder,' Brady said, 'what he, or they, were looking for.'

'Now that,' Linda said, 'is the big question. We've got to hope that it was just money. Of which, I should imagine, they found none. Ironical, isn't it? If they'd come just a bit later he'd have had five hundred dollars. It might have saved his life.'

She took a ball-point pen from her shoulder bag and began sifting through the papers on the bureau. Suddenly she gave a little exclamation of satisfaction.

'Ah!'

Brady had been standing idly by, doing nothing but feeling very much on edge and impatient to get away. Now he saw that Linda had picked an envelope from the heap. He saw also that it was the very one marked with a cross that Ruiz had shown them on the previous day.

'So that's not what they wanted.'

'Apparently not. You can bet now it was just cash. Fortunately for us.'

'And now may we go?'

'Of course.'

She put the envelope in her bag and Brady walked to the door. He was about to grasp the knob in order to pull the door open when she stopped him with a hand on his arm.

'Don't touch it. Fingerprints. Use your handkerchief.'

He took out his handkerchief and wrapped it round the knob before gripping it. He pulled the door halfway open and peered out. There was no one in sight.

'All clear.'

She went out first and he followed, pulling the door shut

after transferring his handkerchief to the outer knob. They went down the stairs warily, making as little sound as possible. They met no one there or in the lobby, and outside in the street the taxi was waiting.

Chapter Eight

BEETLE

'Suppose,' Brady said, 'the police come looking for us.'

'Now why on earth would they do that?' Linda asked.

They had paid off the cab-driver in the centre of town and were having a meal in a restaurant. The food was good, but Brady would have enjoyed it more if the picture of Pedro Ruiz lying dead and bloodied on the floor of his room had not persisted in occupying his mind with all its gruesome detail.

'They'll be investigating the murder as soon as they get to hear about it, and then they'll be hunting for the killer. That's what policemen do you know. It's their job.'

'So?'

'So they'll want to know who paid a call on Ruiz very recently, won't they?'

'Maybe.'

'Well, doesn't that bother you at all?'

'Look, Steve,' she said, 'who saw us go there? That woman yesterday. She doesn't know who we are, and I doubt whether she could give much of a description of us. People seldom can, you know. They're inclined to be pretty vague when called upon to do that sort of thing.'

'How about the cabbies?'

'Same applies to them. They don't know our names. And I can't see either of them running to the coppers and volunteering information anyway. Why should they? It's no skin off their noses, and they won't want to be involved. What good would it do for them?'

He could see there was logic in what she was saying, but he was still not altogether convinced. Stumbling over the body of a murdered man had not been something he had been led to expect when he had been offered this job, and he was not at all happy about it. And what really was the job anyway? That he would very much like to know.

'I think, Linda,' he said, 'it's high time you came clean with me.'

'In what way, Steve?'

'In the way of you telling me just what sort of game it is we're playing. I feel I have a right to know. Don't you agree?'

'Well, yes,' she said, after giving the matter some thought, 'perhaps you do. But it's not a game, you know. Far from it.'

'So what is it? What in fact is Adsum Worldwide's business?'

She hesitated, as though debating in her mind just how much to reveal to him. Then she said: 'I don't know precisely how they would describe themselves; they've never really given me an exact definition, and they don't advertise in the usual way. I suppose you might call them confidential advisers to industry. They have these agents in the field, various parts of the world, and they keep their ears to the ground and pick up information on this and that, which they send in by courier. Adsum then get in touch with some party they think might be interested and pass it on. At a price, of course. At least, that's the way I see it, though it's never actually been spelt out to me. I just take orders and carry them out.'

'As one of the couriers?'

'Yes.'

'Actually what you're talking about is industrial espionage, isn't it?'

'I suppose some people might call it that.'

'What would you call it?'

She hesitated again for a bit. Then she gave a sigh and said: 'Industrial espionage.'

'So in fact you're still in the spy game. You've just got different masters. Is that it?'

She answered a trifle reluctantly: 'In a manner of speaking, yes.' Then she added quickly: 'But I don't do any of the information gathering myself. As I said, I'm just a courier. I contact the agent in the field and carry what's what back to London.'

Brady thought about what she had just told him, and it made him feel even less happy than he had already been feeling. Because it was only too obvious to him that people in industry who had secrets that were worth stealing would be none too keen on letting other people get their fingers on them. It would make them very upset, and they might resort to extreme measures to protect their interests; measures like giving the quietus to anyone they suspected of trying to steal a march on them.

So much for those assurances he had been given that the operation in which he and Linda were engaged entailed no risk. Ruiz was dead already, and though his death might have nothing to do with the Adsum business, then again it just might. It was all very worrying to anyone of a nervous disposition. Such as Stephen Brady, for example.

'I think,' he said, 'this is where I hand in my cards. I think I'll take a seat on the next plane out.'

'You can't do that,' she said.

'Who says I can't?'

'I do,' she said.

'Give me one good reason.'

'It would be breaking your contract.'

'What contract? I don't recall signing anything of that description.'

'Maybe not. But there was a gentlemen's agreement.'

'I'm not a gentleman.'

She resorted to pleading; always a useful ploy. 'But Steve darling, you can't just walk out on me. I need you. There was a catch in her voice and she even managed to bring a tear into her eye. 'You do see that, don't you? How would I manage without you?'

He knew he was sunk then. Because he had never been able to put up much resistance to that kind of pressure from her. He knew it was an act of course, put on for the sole purpose of bringing him to heel; she had used the method so many times before; but act or no act, it always worked.

'OK,' he said. 'You win.'

'So no pulling out?'

'No pulling out. I'm a sucker again. But that's the way it always has been and always will be, I suppose.'

'Oh no, Steve, not a sucker. Just a loyal partner.'

'Same thing, but sounds better. Anyway, I'm still not terribly happy about old Pedro Ruiz. Suppose he was rumbled by the people who are being spied on, and they decided to remove him from circulation. Could be, couldn't it?'

She shook her head. 'Highly unlikely. As I said, he was only a go-between. And whoever killed him left the envelope behind without even looking inside it. My guess still is that the intruder, or intruders, were in a different business; probably drug traffickers he owed money to. Maybe they'd come to collect the debt, and when Ruiz refused to pay them, or just couldn't, they turned nasty and gave him the knife. *Pour encourager les autres*, as the saying is.'

'I daresay you're right. But there's something else that puzzles me. Why, for Pete's sake, in a country like Paraguay, is there any industrial secret that would be worth stealing?'

'Who knows? Stranger things do happen. Anyway, that's not our concern. All we have to do is contact our Mr Garfield and take what he has to give us. It's as simple as that.'

Harold Garfield was the name on the slip of paper that had been inside the buff envelope. There was an address as well, but it was not in Asunción. They would have been surprised if it had been.

'There's one thing,' Brady said. 'Whoever snuffed out friend Pedro saved you five hundred dollars. We might as well have taken the envelope from him yesterday after all. It would have made no difference to him. He was for the high jump anyway.'

'But it would still have been dishonest.'

Brady gave a laugh. 'As if this whole operation wasn't as dishonest as cheating at cards!'

She made no answer to that.

After they had finished their meal they did not set out at once to find Mr Garfield. Linda said it would be best to leave it until the next day because there were a few things to attend to in Asunción first.

One of these was to buy a gun.

When Linda told him this Brady felt another little tremor in his nervous system, which had scarcely recovered from the Pedro Ruiz business.

'So you're expecting trouble?'

'Not expecting it, no. But one should be prepared for anything in a country like this.'

'Such as the need of a gun?'

'Yes.'

They found a gunshop without much difficulty. It was in a narrow side-street and sold hunting-knives and fishing tackle and camping gear and a lot of other stuff besides. It was rather dark in the shop, and there was a curious odour; a mixture of new leather and gun-oil and hemp and other unidentifiable ingredients. There was a long wooden counter, and behind it were racks of sporting rifles and shotguns of various kinds. Brady could see no machine-guns, but he would not have been surprised if these could be supplied on request.

In charge of this display of lethal hardware was a stringy little wisp of a man with a mat of greying hair and a face like an Egyptian mummy's. When Brady and Linda walked up to the counter he glanced briefly at the woman before turning his attention to the man, evidently assuming that he was the prospective customer. Linda demonstrated to him that he was under an illusion in this respect by asking to be shown some handguns.

'Not too heavy.'

With a faintly disbelieving air the man fished out from beneath the counter a selection of small-calibre self-loading pistols and revolvers. Linda ignored the revolvers and finally settled for a .25 calibre Smith & Wesson self-loader. The salesman watched her closely as she handled it, still with that expression of faint disbelief on his mummy-like face. Brady wondered whether she was the first woman who had come to

him for a gun. In a country like Paraguay it seemed hardly
likely.

She ordered some ammunition and filled a clip and slipped it
into the butt of the pistol. The practised manner in which she
did this came as no surprise to Brady. Years ago he had seen her
use just such a weapon to good effect on more than one occasion. In those days she had been in the habit of carrying a
Beretta in her shoulder bag, and no doubt this gun would be put
in the same place.

She turned to Brady. 'Sure you don't want a gun too?'

'Absolutely.'

If he had had one, where would he have carried it? In a
pocket? That sort of thing was awkward in the normal pocket;
too heavy and too bulky. Stuck in the waistband of the trousers
it was uncomfortable and tended to be conspicuous and attract
unwanted attention. There were such things as shoulder
holsters, but he had never worn one and was not prepared to
start now. And besides, why would he need a gun? Had he not
been assured that there was no danger whatever in this job he
was doing? Not, of course, that he believed one word of that
now. Nevertheless, if there was to be any shooting – and he
fervently hoped there would not be – he preferred to leave that
side of the business to his companion. She had had more prac-
tice at it than he had.

'Well,' she said, 'please yourself.'

She paid for the pistol and the ammunition and stowed both
in her shoulder bag, as Brady had expected.

'Ready now?' he asked. 'You don't want a Bowie knife to
complete the armament?'

'Don't be sarcastic,' she said. 'It doesn't suit you. Now let's
go.'

The stringy man with the mummy-like face watched then leave. He still seemed bemused by the fact that of the pair it had been the woman who had bought the gun, while the man had just stood by. It had probably been a unique event in his experience.

They had decided, though in fact the decision had been Linda's and Brady had simply agreed with it, that they needed a car. According to the information on the note in the buff envelope, Harold Garfield was apparently hanging out at a place called Acapurno, which reference to a map of the country indicated was some one hundred and fifty kilometres roughly north-north-west of Asunción. It did not appear to be a very large town, and no one had seen fit to build a railway connecting it with other parts of the state. It was unlikely that there would be an airline link between it and the capital either; so the only way of getting there had to be by road. There might possibly have been some kind of bus service, but even if this were so, a car seemed preferable.

'There's bound to be a rental firm here, I should imagine,' Linda said. 'We'll have a look.'

They made enquiries and were directed to an establishment where they were assured they would find what they were looking for. It was in fact a branch of a firm known world-wide, but in the event they never reached it; they were diverted on the way there.

The cause of this diversion was a concrete forecourt on which were parked several used cars with prices displayed on their windscreens. Brady would have passed by with scarcely a glance, but Linda came to a stop and he was forced to stop too.

'Now I wonder,' she said.

She was looking at the cars, and there could have been only one thought in her head. To Brady it seemed crazy.

'Surely you're not thinking of buying one of these?'

'There might be advantages.'

'There'd certainly be disadvantages. These are probably a load of clapped-out old junk.'

'Well, there's no harm in taking a closer look.'

She stepped on to the forecourt, and again he was obliged to follow suit. As if by magic a salesman appeared from the building at the rear. He was of a type Brady would have distrusted on sight: dark-suited, slicked-down black hair shining like a polished shoe, sideburns, thin moustache, moist lips. He could have played the villain, or indeed the hero, in any number of Hollywood films of the twenties or thirties.

'You are looking for a car?' he said. There was an oily quality about his voice, and when he smiled he revealed a set of teeth like brand new gravestones without the lettering.

The question was superfluous. They had certainly not come there to gather flowers.

'Perhaps,' Linda said.

'You are American.'

'No. British.'

It seemed to disappoint him a little. Possibly his anticipation of a profitable sale had taken a slight knock. But he quickly perked up again and began to extol the virtues of a number of the vehicles on display. Linda, however, gave them only a cursory glance; her eyes appeared to be caught by a red Volkswagen Beetle. She walked over to it, with Brady and the salesman following in her wake. It had not taken the black-haired man long to guess which of the two was the potential buyer.

It was obvious that the Beetle was old and had clocked up a lot of miles in its time. There were dents and scratches here and there in the bodywork, but no rust to speak of, and the tyres were not too bad. The upholstery had suffered from wear and tear, but that was only to be expected. There was a price on the windscreen: it was a colossal number of Paraguayan guaranis, but it was marked in American dollars also and this looked a far more reasonable sum at four hundred units of the US currency.

'This is in running order?' Linda asked.

The salesman assured her that it was. 'Ready to drive away with no trouble at all.'

'We should require a demonstration run.'

The man shrugged. 'Naturally.'

Brady stared at Linda, aghast. 'You're not seriously thinking of buying this?'

'Why not? It's cheap.'

'But it's an old banger. It would probably break down and leave us stranded miles from anywhere.'

'I don't see why it should, I used to drive one of these years ago. They're built to last.'

'But not for ever.'

'Steve,' she said, 'as I've told you before, you worry too much. We'll give it a try.'

She drove, with the salesman sitting beside her and Brady in the back. The Beetle was rather noisy, but that was to be expected considering the age of the beast. They did not go far; but it was far enough for Linda to make a decision to buy. She haggled and got the price down to $350, with a full tank of petrol and the necessary documentation.

Brady still thought it was madness, but it made no difference. It was Miss Manning who was calling the shots.

Chapter Nine

STRANGERS IN TOWN

She let him drive part the way. He had never driven a Beetle before, but he soon got the hang of it. There was some back-lash on the steering and the noise level got pretty high if you pushed the speed up much above sixty kilometres per hour; but they were in no hurry, so this hardly mattered.

The road was not too bad for the first forty kilometres or so, though it would hardly have matched even a B class road in England. Then they came to a town marked on the map as Mendoza. It was of no great size, and since it was of no interest to them they drove straight through it. On the other side the road they had to take was really bad; it was unmetalled and full of potholes and ruts, over which the Beetle made its way, bumping and shuddering as though possessed by a devil. The jarring was enough to make Brady's teeth ache, and he had a fear that something vital would surely break – possibly the back axle. But Linda seemed unperturbed.

They passed through villages that were no more than a few adobe hovels, all jumbled together as though for mutual protection. Dogs barked at them as they drove by, and ragged children turned to stare as at some creature from another planet. There was little other traffic; though now and then they would meet a lorry with crates and sacks and miscellaneous other gear piled high on the back, the odd pick-up truck or battered car or a man riding on a mule.

'I hope,' Brady said, 'your Mr Garfield is not bringing us on a wild-goose chase.'

'He is not *my* Mr Garfield,' she said, rather snappishly. 'And why would he be doing anything like that? Where would be the point of the exercise?'

It was a warm day, dry, with only a few wispy clouds in the sky. To the west the land stretched away to the distant horizon with little to see but coarse grass and a few clumps of stunted trees here and there. Some cattle could be seen in the distance, but to Brady it seemed poor grazing.

'It's as well,' Linda said, 'we didn't come in the rainy season. I'm told that these dirt roads just turn to mud.'

'That must be nice. Floods too, I suppose.'

'Very likely. As it is, we're coming up to that time of the year, and we may get a storm or two if we're unlucky.'

'Now you've really cheered me up.'

It took them almost four hours to reach Acapurno; and when Brady saw the place he wondered why anyone would ever bother to make the journey. Everything about it seemed to be on a small scale: there was a small church and a small inn and a small central square, which the inhabitants probably called a plaza and maybe some other word in the Guarani language, which Linda told him more than half the natives still spoke.

They went to the inn first, because they were hungry and thought it the most likely place where a meal would be obtainable. It was on the edge of the plaza, and that was where they parked the Beetle, along with a few other cars and a couple of pick-up trucks, all of which were shabby enough not to make the Beetle seem out of place.

In the inn there appeared to be only one public room, which served both as a bar and a diner. There was just one long table, at which three men were having a meal, while two others were at the bar drinking beer. Behind the counter was a fat swarthy man with shirt-sleeves rolled up to reveal massive forearms as hairy as the chest which was visible in the opening of the shirt. Brady made a guess that this was the landlord, and it was to him that he addressed his enquiry as to the availability of a meal. Later he was to learn that the man's name was Cortés, like the conqueror of Mexico.

From the moment that he and Linda had entered the room the eyes of all those already there had been on them, as though they had been exotic creatures such as had never been seen in those parts before. Perhaps strangers in town were a rarity and worthy of more than a second glance.

In answer to the question the innkeeper admitted that meals were indeed served in the place. He seemed to do so with some reluctance, but he could hardly have denied the fact when there were three men at the table already dining.

'You wish to eat?'

Brady replied that this was their wish. 'We have come a long way and are hungry. What can we have?'

He was not expecting a wide choice, which was just as well, since the only alternative to a kind of stew appeared to be bread and cheese. They chose the stew, which was served by a stout, black-haired woman who turned out to be the landlord's wife and appeared from a kitchen at the rear of the bar. She was also the cook and was assisted by a slatternly girl who was a kind of maid of all work.

The stew was better than might have been expected, and they ate it at the long table from which the three other diners soon departed.

'I wonder what's in this,' Brady said.

'Perhaps it would be advisable not to enquire,' Linda said. 'Just eat it and be thankful.'

Before leaving the inn they asked if they could be directed to the address where Harold Garfield was supposed to be living. The innkeeper was able to give the necessary directions, but Brady thought he appeared rather surprised by the question, as though he would not have expected two people like them to be going to such an address.

'Is it far?'

'No, not far. You will find it easily.'

'Thank you,' Brady said. 'Thank you for your help.'

The man shrugged. 'It is nothing.'

They decided to leave the car in the plaza and walk. It was, as the innkeeper had said, not far; no more than a quarter of a mile at most. It was on the northern outskirts of the town on a piece of waste ground beyond the last of the houses. It was what in the United States would have been called a trailer park; in Britain a caravan site. It was in a hollow and they came to it along a rough track sloping downward. It had the shabby, down-at-heel appearance that such settlements all too often have. There was no order about it; the caravans were parked here and there, some pointing in one direction, some in another.

Brady had often wondered why caravans always seemed to be white; it made them stand out from the background in all their stark unsightliness. Surely if they had been painted green they would have blended more comfortably into the surroundings.

'So this it,' Linda said, in a tone of disgust. 'What a dump.'

There was litter everywhere. There was washing hung on lines. Scruffy dogs wandered around, looking for anything to eat, or lay sleeping in the sun. Near a patch of scrub on the far side a goat was tethered. The place was limited in size, and there were no more than a dozen caravans all told. The amount seemed greater because of the way they were scattered around, and the mess their occupants had made was out of all proportion to their numbers. Some ragged children were playing around and making the kind of high-pitched sounds that children were in the habit of making.

'This is hardly the sort of base I should have expected an Adsum agent to be using,' Brady said.

'And yet,' Linda said, 'why not? Here he's free to come and go without anyone taking much notice. People here probably mind their own business and don't pry too much into their neighbours' affairs.'

The truth of this seemed to be borne out when they asked one or two people to direct them to Garfield's van and were met with a blank stare or a shake of the head. But finally a young woman with a baby on her arm said: 'Oh, you mean the gringo.' And she pointed out a caravan at the scrubby end of the site, some way from the nearest of the others, as if it had a wish to keep its distance from the neighbours. 'That is where he lives, but I do not think he is at home just now because his car is not there.'

'All the same,' Linda said, 'I think we will go and see. He may be there.'

They walked over to the caravan and knocked on the door; and when this brought no response Brady tried the handle but found that it was locked.

'So what now?' he said. 'Do we stick around and hope he soon comes back?'

Linda was not in favour of this, and Brady agreed with her. It was not the kind of place where he would have chosen to wait. They did not fit in and there were no seats available. There were three steps leading up to the door of Garfield's caravan, and they might have sat on one of these, but it would have been cramped and uncomfortable.

'I think it would be best,' Linda said, 'if we were to go back to the inn to see whether it's possible to get a room for the night. There's no telling when Garfield will turn up, and I don't fancy a late drive back to Asunción on that road. It could be hell in the dark.'

'I agree. We don't know what the Beetle's lights are like and it might break down.'

She ignored this remark. On the subject of the car's reliability she was inclined to be a trifle sensitive. It had been her purchase and she had complete faith in it. Brady had to admit that so far this faith appeared to have been well founded; there had been no hint of a breakdown on the road from Asunción. But there was yet time.

They left the caravans and walked back to the inn. There were a few more customers at the bar, but nobody was eating a meal. The man with the hairy forearms appeared surprised to see them again. He was even more surprised when Brady asked whether they could have a room for the night. But he did not deny that there was a room available.

'May we see it?'

'If you wish.'

They were conducted to the room by Señora Cortès, who had earlier served them with lunch. It was on the first floor and was better than Brady had feared it might be. It was small and sparely furnished, but it was clean, with whitewashed walls and a window overlooking the Plaza where the red beetle could be seen in its parking place.

The woman stood with hands on hips as they made a cursory inspection of the room. Then: 'Is it satisfactory?'

It was Linda who answered: 'Yes. It will do very nicely.'

'How long do you wish to stay?'

'Perhaps only the one night; possibly longer. That will be convenient?'

The woman shrugged. 'Why not?' She seemed neither pleased nor otherwise. Her face was expressionless, and Brady would have guessed from the look of her that she had more of the native Guarani blood in her veins than that of the Spanish conquerors.

Their accommodation for the duration of their stay in Acapurno, which Brady sincerely hoped would not be extensive, having been thus arranged, they moved the Beetle to a yard at the rear of the inn and transferred their luggage to the room. Then, to pass the time, they took a stroll round the town, which, it had to be admitted, had little in the way of tourist attractions. There was no bank, but there was a garage with petrol pumps and a few small shops. The only evidence that civilization had reached this outpost was a Coca-Cola sign outside the garage. The Big Mac appeared not yet to have arrived.

For a while they sat on a bench under a shady tree in the

plaza, watching the world, such as it was in Acapurna, go by. And this, Brady remarked was the next best thing to watching paint dry.

'I thought,' Linda said, 'that this was what you liked. No excitment. Nothing to heat the blood.'

'You may be right at that. But why is it, I wonder, that when things are all as quiet as a nice secluded grave I always feel that just around the corner fate may be waiting with a hammer in its hand ready to give me an almighty wallop on the nut.'

'It's the way you're made, Steve. You have a nervous disposition. Anyway, there's no cause to worry. Once we've contacted Garfield and picked up whatever it is he has for us we'll be on our way home, and that will be that.'

'I wouldn't bet on it,' Brady said. 'I just wouldn't bet on it.'

Chapter Ten

NOT OUT OF THE WOOD

Later in the afternoon they took another walk out to the caravan site. No luck. Garfield still had not returned.

'Damn the man,' Linda said. She sounded really annoyed. 'Where can he have got to? He should have been here to meet us.'

'But he wouldn't have known we were coming on this particular day,' Brady reminded her. 'You couldn't expect him to hang around day after day in a wretched spot like this just on the off-chance that we would turn up.'

'Well, it's a damned nuisance anyway. I just hope nothing's happpened to him.'

'Like what, for instance?'

'Oh, I don't know. Anything.'

'Like what happened to the late and not much lamented Pedro Ruiz, do you mean?'

'No, I don't,' she answered quickly. 'That was an unconnected incident and there's no reason to suppose Garfield would be targeted by the same people.'

'Or other people, maybe?'

'No,' she said. 'No. Forget it.'

Which on Brady's part was easier to say than to do. The mental picture of Pedro Ruiz lying on the floor of his wretched little room in Asunción, all bloody and as dead as could be, would persist in returning to haunt him.

They hung around for a while in the hope that the elusive Mr Harold Garfield might turn up; but when, after some fifteen minutes, he had not done so, they decided to return to their temporary base, the inn. They had eaten nothing since lunch, and it was now evening, so they decided to have a meal before paying yet another visit to the agent's caravan.

The meal was rather makeshift, but hunger being the best sauce, they ate it with enjoyment. They were at the coffee stage when the American came across to the table and introduced himself.

They had noticed him when they came in. He was sitting on a stool by the bar, and he was conspicuous by being so different in appearance from anyone else there. He was lean and rather tall, with a craggy face and very fair hair cut *en brosse*, so that it resembled a brand-new coir doormat. He was wearing faded jeans and a short denim jacket and on his feet a pair of scuffed moccasin-type shoes. At a guess Brady would have put his age at somewhere between thirty-five and forty. Overall he gave the impression of being what his countrymen might have described as a tough cookie.

When he reached the table he said: 'Hi there! I hope you folks'll pardon the intrusion, but would I be correct in guessing you're English?'

'You would,' Linda said.

'Just knew it. Felt sure I couldn't be wrong. My name's Petersen. Rex Petersen.'

'Don't tell me,' Linda said. 'You're American. From God's own country.' There was a faint note of mockery in her voice, but Petersen, if he even noticed it, evidently took no offence.

'Right in one. You here on business or pleasure?'

'Maybe a little of each. It's an interesting country, don't you think? And you?'

'Me. Oh, I'm collecting material for a feature in the *National Geographic*. Photographs and stuff. I guess you know the kinda thing.'

'On Paraguay?'

'Sure. Why not?'

'Oh, I don't know. Somehow it doesn't seem like something they would go for.'

'Hey!' Petersen said. 'You just told me it was an interesting country. You changed your mind?'

'Well—'

Seeing her embarrassment, Brady chipped in. He was not sure he accepted Petersen's story either, though he could see no good reason why the man should be lying.

'Have you got a room here too? In the inn, I mean.'

Petersen shook his head. 'Not me. I take my room around with me. It's got four wheels and an engine at the front.'

'A motor caravan?'

'You could call it that, I guess.'

'Sounds like a good idea. Wherever you happen to be, you're still at home sweet home.'

'That's the beauty of it,' Petersen said. 'It gives you independence, if you see what I mean. Anytime the fancy takes hold you can up stakes and be on the move. It's a great feeling.'

He stayed around for a while, talking of this and that, not giving much away regarding himself and not getting much in return either, apart from their names. Finally he stood up, took his leave of them and left the inn.

It was some time later when they themselves left in order to take another walk down to the caravan site. Daylight was beginning to fade, but they could see what they took to be Petersen's travelling home parked on one side of the plaza. They had seen it when they returned to the inn, but had taken little notice of it then. Now they saw that a light was on inside, though curtains drawn across the windows would have made it impossible for anyone to see what was in there.

'Looks as if our American friend values his privacy,' Brady remarked. 'Do you think he really is doing a feature for the *National Geographic*?'

'I doubt it,' Linda said.

'So why would he say he was?'

'Well, my experience is that when people tell you they're doing something which they aren't it's usually because they want to hide what they're really up to.'

'Like us.'

'Just so. Like us.'

'So what would you say his real reason is for being out here?'

'I haven't a clue,' Linda said.

There were lights showing in most of the caravans when they reached the site for the third time, but Garfield's van was dark, and even in the dusk they could see that there was no car near it.

Linda made no attempt to hide her exasperation. 'This really is getting beyond a joke. How many more times do we have to come out here before we find him in?'

'Maybe he's had an accident.'

'That would be just fine, wouldn't it? We travel all this way to see the man and he's in hospital.'

'Or the morgue.'

'Oh, great!'

'It was only a suggestion. Maybe he's with a woman.'

'He's got no business to be. He should be here.'

Brady left it at that. They hung around, feeling that if they went away again their man might arrive just a moment later. Half an hour passed, and it grew steadily darker and more chilly. Brady noticed that Linda was shivering.

'We could make an early night of it and come back first thing in the morning,' he suggested. An early night with Linda Manning was not without its attractions.

She made no response to this suggestion, however; so maybe she was not so attracted to the idea as he was. Which, in his view, was a pity.

Ten more minutes passed.

'Oh bloody hell!' she said. 'Let's go.'

They had gone no more than twenty paces when they heard the sound of a car and saw the headlights swing through a wide arc as it turned on to the track leading down to the caravan site. A moment later they were caught in the beam, and they stepped aside to let the vehicle go past. It appeared to be one of the Range Rover type, which would have been well suited to the local road system. They watched it come to a halt beside Garfield's caravan; and then the lights were switched off and a man got out.

Linda walked up to him and said: 'Mr Garfield?'

He peered at her in the gloom, and she must have been little more than a vague shape to him. 'Who are you?' He sounded nervous.

'My name's Manning,' Linda said. 'And this is Mr Brady. We're from Adsum. You are Mr Garfield, aren't you?'

'Ah!' he said. And he seemed relieved; as if he had feared they might have been less welcome visitors. 'Yes, I'm Garfield. You'd better come inside.'

He went up the steps to the door of the caravan, unlocked it with a key from his pocket and pushed it open. He went inside and he must have been fumbling for a switch, for a moment or two later there was a click and the light came on. Now able to see their way, Linda and Brady followed him in.

'Shut the door,' Garfield said.

Brady did so, while Garfield himself quickly drew the curtains to make sure that no one could look in on them. He still seemed nervous, and Brady wondered why.

'We have been waiting for you,' Linda said; and she made it sound like a complaint. 'This is our third visit.'

'I'm sorry,' Garfield said. 'If I'd known you were coming today—' He made a motion with his hands, a gesture of mute apology. 'I didn't think it would have taken quite so long.'

He was, Brady imagined, referring to their journey from London. No doubt he had been waiting impatiently for their arrival and wondering what was delaying them.

He was a small man, little more than five feet six inches in height and sparely built. He was round-shouldered, with lank brown hair, slightly greasy and receding from the forehead. His face was pinched, cheeks sunken, giving him an almost haggard look. He seemed tired and he could have used a shave. He was wearing fawn cotton trousers and a rather dirty gaberdine zipper jacket. On his feet he had a pair of well-worn trainers. Taken all in all, he was far from being an impressive sort of individual. Certainly not in Brady's estimation. But appearances could of course be deceptive, and it was possible that this Harold Garfield might in fact be a pretty hot number. He doubted it, but it was possible.

Linda repudiated the implied suggestion that they had been dragging their feet in responding to the signal he had sent to London.

'These matters can't be arranged overnight, you know. Anyway, we're here now, and that's the main thing.'

Garfield admitted that this was so. And then, as if suddenly calling to mind his obligations as a host, he invited them to sit down and offered to make some coffee.

Brady thought Linda was going to reject the offer and insist on getting straight down to business, but after a slight hesitation she said: 'OK. Coffee will be fine.'

The furnishing of the caravan was fairly basic; it was certainly no luxury mobile home and it looked as though it had seen a lot of use, probably by a succession of other occupants before its present one. There were settees on each side, which probably doubled as beds, and there was a small table. At one end was what served as a kitchen; it had a sink and a cooking-stove that used bottled gas as fuel. A number of small lockers provided storage facilities.

Garfield filled a kettle and lit a gas ring to heat the water. He found three mugs and spooned instant coffee from a jar.

'You take sugar, milk?' he asked. 'Evaporated, I'm afraid.'

'I'll have mine black,' Linda said. 'And no sugar.'

Brady settled for sugar and tinned milk. He hoped the mugs were clean, but there was a dingy look about the whole interior of the caravan that did not give him much confidence on this point. He doubted whether in Garfield's book hygiene figured at all prominently.

Nothing much was said as the coffee was being made, but when Garfield had handed out the steaming mugs he hauled a battered packet of cigarettes from a pocket and offered them to Linda. She refused, and Brady also rejected the offer. He had given up smoking years ago, and when he saw what it did to your lungs he felt no inclination to take it up again.

Garfield seemed inclined to take one of the cigarettes for himself, but then decided not to when he saw the disapproving expression on Miss Manning's face, and he stowed the packet away again.

'Before we get down to business,' Linda said, 'there's something I think you ought to know. It concerns your man in Asunción.'

Garfield's head jerked up, as though he were anticipating something unpleasant. 'Pedro Ruiz?'

'Yes.'

'He's not in trouble, is he?'

'No; not any more. He's past that. He's dead. Murdered.'

'Oh, my God!' Garfield said. And he looked really shocked. 'How did it happen?'

'Maybe you'd better have that cigarette after all,' Linda said. 'You may need it to steady your nerves.'

'Yes,' Garfield said. He retrieved the packet, took a cigarette from it and lit it with a match. Brady noticed that his hands were shaking. The news of Ruiz's death seemed to have taken him quite off balance. 'How?'

'It happened this way., We went to see him the day before yesterday. And I must say that room of his was just the pits; an absolute pigsty and no mistake.'

Garfield nodded. 'He had rather let things slide this last year or so.'

'I can believe it. Well, he had your name and address in an envelope but wouldn't let us have it unless we paid him five hundred dollars. And as we didn't have the cash right then and there we said we'd get it and come back the next day.'

'He had no right to demand any money. He'd already been paid by me.'

'Is that so? No doubt he spent it soon enough. Seems like he needed lots of money to pay for that junk he was shooting into his arm.'

'Did he tell you that?'

'No. But he didn't need to. We could see. So we left him and picked up the money next day – yesterday, that is – and went back and found him lying on the floor, dead as mutton.'

'How was he killed?'

'Stabbed. He'd bled a lot. The room had been searched, but fortunately the envelope with your address was still in the desk.'

Garfield drew on his cigarette and let the smoke come out with his words. 'The police? They weren't there?'

'No. Nobody was.'

'Did you report what you found?'

'Of course not. You think we want to get ourselves involved in a thing like that? Talk sense.'

'I guess not.' He dragged at the cigarette again. 'I wonder who could have killed him.'

'The way we figure it,' Linda said, 'is that it was probably somebody in the drug trade he owed money to. Got tired of waiting for him to cough up and decided to cross him off the books.'

Garfield seemed happy to go along with this. It meant that whoever had put Ruiz out of circulation would not be looking for him as the next victim. However, the very fact that he felt his own life might be in danger did not please Brady at all. It failed to fit in with those assurances he had been given that the operation he was engaged in entailed no risk whatever to life or limb. But he had already given up believing that anyway. Harold Garfield's all too apparent nervousness merely served to strengthen his disbelief. Still, he and Linda would soon be out of it and on their way home, so there was really no reason for any misgiving, was there?

And then, as if to confirm this reassuring thought, Linda drained her coffee cup, set it down on the table and said: 'Right then, Mr Garfield, all we need now is for you to hand over whatever it is you have for us, and that'll be the end of the business.'

Garfield squirmed; there could be no other word for it. He appeared most uncomfortable and he avoided looking Miss Manning straight in the eye. When he spoke it was in a strangled sort of voice, as though he had difficulty forcing the words out.

'I'm sorry,' he said, 'but I'm afraid it's not quite as simple as that.'

And Brady guessed then that they were not yet out of the wood. Not by a long chalk.

Chapter Eleven

EXCURSION

'What do you mean, not as simple as that?' Linda demanded. And she turned on the hapless Garfield what Brady could only describe in his own mind as a gimlet eye. And a very sharp gimlet at that.

'I haven't got it yet,' Garfield said. And he looked, if that were possible, even more embarrassed than he had been before.

'Haven't got it yet! But I was led to believe by Adsum that you had been in touch with them and had reported that you had some very important information waiting to be picked up. Why else would we be here?'

'Well—'

'Did you or did you not tell them that?'

'Yes, but—'

'Why?'

'I thought I would have it by the time you got here.'

'What made you think that?'

'I'd been promised it would be.'

'Promised by whom?'

Brady liked that 'whom'. It demonstrated that, however infuriated she might be, Miss Manning was not forgetful of her grammar.

'By this man,' Garfield said.

'What man, for heaven's sake? Does he have a name?'

'Yes. Carlos.'

'Just Carlos? Nothing more?'

'That's all he would tell me. It may not be his real name either.'

'Oh, fine! Somebody with a false name promises to hand you some red-hot information, and on the strength of that you contact London and ask them to send someone hotfoot to pick it up.'

'I didn't want to waste time. I felt sure he'd deliver. He was going to be paid, and he seemed the sort who would do anything for money.'

'Did you give him any?'

'A little. On account.'

'And you haven't seen him since?'

'No.'

'I've never heard anything like this,' Linda said. 'Never. Are you crazy or just plain bloody stupid?'

Brady put a word in. 'What made you think this Carlos was the real McCoy?'

'There's this place where he works, you see. I've had my eye on it for some time. That's why I moved out here. It seems worth investigating.'

'What place would that be?'

'It's out in the wilds, quite a way from here. But I don't think there's much point in talking about it right now. What I suggest is tomorrow we go and have a look at it. You'll see then why it caught my attention. There's something here worth following up. I'm sure of it.'

'There'd better be,' Linda said. 'Otherwise, my friend, you're in deep trouble. They're not going to be at all pleased at Adsum headquarters if we go back empty-handed. They'll have handed out good money all for nothing, and nobody likes doing that.'

Brady could see that she was falling in with Garfield's suggestion, and he was none too happy about this. It meant that they would be hanging around for another day at least, and he would rather have been on the way out first thing in the morning. He just hoped the postponement would be for no more than a day, but he was not banking on it; he knew that Linda would be reluctant to return to London with nothing to show for this Paraguayan operation.

'OK then,' she said. 'Let's say nine o'clock tomorrow morning. And you provide the transport. Right?'

'Right,' Garfield said.

They arrived dead on time at Garfield's caravan in the morning, having walked from the inn. In daylight they could see that his car was not in fact a Range Rover but one of the cheaper four-wheel-drive, off-the-road vehicles that originated in the Far East: a Mitsubishi Shogun, and not a very new one at that; it looked as if it had done a deal of work in its time. It also appeared that Garfield was not one of those proud owners who were forever busy with the wash-leather and the polish. There was a drab, neglected look about the car, and there was dried mud on the wheels. In a way, Brady reflected, it pretty well matched its owner, who was a fairly drab sort of individual himself.

He came out of the caravan as they approached. He had probably spotted them from one of the windows and was ready to go. He was dressed in the same clothes as he had been wearing the previous evening, and maybe he had slept in them. He had shaved, but had made rather a poor job of it and had cut himself just below the chin. It looked as though he had stanched the flow of blood with cotton wool, and there was some of it adhering to the skin.

'So you're here,' he said.

It was a pretty inane remark, and Linda answered with a touch of acidity: 'What did you expect? That we wouldn't turn up?'

He gave a weak smile. 'No, of course not. Hardly likely, was it? I mean this is all in your interest, isn't it?'

'And in yours.'

'Yes, mine too of course. We're all in this together, aren't we?'

He seemed nervous, Brady thought. Perhaps it was his normal state, or perhaps the death of Pedro Ruiz and the violent manner of it was still preying on his mind.

They got into the Shogun, Garfield and Linda in the front and Brady riding in the back. There was a good deal of activity at the caravan site as the inhabitants prepared for whatever it was that occupied their time during the day. Whatever this might be, none of them appeared to be getting very rich from the exercise. If they had been, it was hardly likely that they would have remained in such a dump.

'How long have you been living in this place?' Linda asked.

'Not long,' Garfield said. 'It's just temporary.'

'You were in Asunción before?'

'Yes. I'll probably go back there as soon as this business is cleared up.'

He drove the Shogun up the track from the hollow and on to the road. Here he turned to the right and headed in the direction that would take them away from the town and into country unfamiliar to his passengers. It was a continuation of that same road by which they had journeyed from Asunción, no better and no worse; the kind of surface to which the Shogun was more suited than the Beetle had been.

'How far is this place you're taking us to?' Linda asked.

'About sixty kilometres,' Garfield said.

'And it's all like this? The road, I mean.'

'In parts it's worse. There are some fine tarmacked highways in Paraguay, but they don't run out to these parts. Maybe some day these roads wil be improved, but not yet awhile. Development is mostly to the east. That's what makes what you're going to see so amazing. It just doesn't fit in.'

'So what is it?'

'You'll see,' Garfield said.

And that was as much as he seemed prepared to divulge for the present.

They passed through no towns on the way; nothing but a small village here and there. But the road had to lead somewhere, Brady reflected, so perhaps eventually they would reach another town, even if it was no more impressive than Acapurno. But they had still not arrived at any such place when, after some forty kilometres of rough going, they came to a point where another road branched off to the left at an angle of roughly thirty degrees.

There was no signpost; nothing whatever to indicate whither this side-road led. But Garfield unhesitatingly steered the Shogun on to it. Rather surprisingly, it was in rather better condition than the one they had left. There were not so many potholes, and it appeared to be much less used. Linda remarked on this, and Garfield gave an explanation.

'This road is a lot newer than the other one, and it doesn't take a great deal of traffic. Very little, in fact.'

'Why is that?'

'Because there's only one place it leads to, and uninvited visitors are not exactly welcome there.'

'There was no sign at the junction to tell people this is a private road.'

'No need. Nobody's going to come down here just to look at the scenery.'

This seemed true enough; the scenery was certainly not much to look at. There were some low, bare hills in the distance, a few stunted trees here and there, a lot of barren ground, some of it so marshy that the road-builders had been forced to make wide detours, no sign of life. A word came into Brady's mind to describe it, and the word was desolate. He wondered whether this journey was really necessary, but he knew that Linda would maintain that it was.

They had been travelling for some time, with Garfield not pushing the Shogun but maintaining a steady speed of rather more than sixty kilometres per hour when they came to a point where the road began to slope gently upwards for some distance. Ahead, on the left, a fairly extensive area of scrub extended to the summit of this low hill. It stretched along the skyline; dark, and to Brady's way of thinking, more than a little sinister.

'How much further is it?' Linda asked.

'Not far now,' Garfield said. 'Nearly there.'

A little later he brought the car to a halt.

'Why have you stopped?' Linda demanded.

'Because now we have a choice. Do we drive on and approach openly what lies ahead or do we reconnoitre from a distance without revealing ourselves? My advice is that we exercise caution and take the latter course.'

Brady could tell that he was on edge. He had certainly been there before and felt uneasy; perhaps with good reason. He was obviously hoping that Linda would opt for the cautious approach, and after some hesitation she did.

'I fail to see what there is to fear,' she said, 'but there will be no harm in looking before we leap.'

'Then I'll just take the car off the road,' Garfield said. 'We don't want it to be conspicuous, do we?'

There was a verge of about ten yards between the road and the scrub, and he drove the Shogun over this and in among the stunted trees and thorn bushes, twigs and small branches scraping the sides of the vehicle. When it had penetrated far enough to be out of sight from the road he brought it to a halt and switched off the ignition.

'From here,' he said, 'we have to walk.'

He took a pair of binoculars from the glove compartment and they all got out. With him in the lead they then began to thread their way through the scrub, heading towards the summit of the hill. It was not easy going; there were thorns and brambles to contend with, but the distance was not great, and soon they came to the end of the climb. In front of them now the ground dropped away rather more steeply and there was little growth to obstruct the view.

'Look,' Garfield said.

In front of them was a hollow, rather like a vast amphitheatre. And in this bowl, contrasting sharply with all the natural wilderness surrounding it, was something that had not been fashioned by the hand of nature but by that of man: an industrial establishment.

At least, that was what it looked like.

'Wow!' Linda said.

Garfield handed her the binoculars. 'Take a look through these.'

She did so. She took a long look, and then handed the glasses to Brady. 'This is certainly interesting, don't you think?'

He put the binoculars to his eyes and the whole layout in the hollow seemed to jump towards him. And interesting was rather an understatement for what he was seeing. There were some long, low buildings that could have been constructed of concrete near the centre, and some distance away from them were a lot of smaller ones which might have been living quarters. In addition there was an erection of pipes and metal tanks that looked like some kind of refinery. A thin column of smoke or steam was rising from it and dispersing in the air.

There was a perimeter fence of chain-link netting surrounding the place, topped by what appeared to be razor-wire, and the entire surface within the fence was tarmacked. People were moving around in this enclosure, and there were some lorries and other vehicles, as well as a couple of fork-lift trucks, some parked, some in motion.

He could see where the road came down to a gateway in the fence, and here there was a kind of gatekeeper's hut at one side. The gate was closed, and he did not doubt that it was locked.

'Doesn't look as if they encourage visitors,' he remarked.

'They don't,' Garfield said.

'Are you speaking from experience?'

'Yes. There's an armed guard on the gate, and you'd need to, have a very good reason for being allowed in.'

'Then I don't think I'll bother,' Brady said.

He handed the binoculars back to Garfield, who slung them on his shoulder by the strap.

And that was when they heard the sound of the helicopter approaching.

Chapter Twelve

LIKE THE OLD DAYS

It came from the further side of the enclosure and it was flying low. It was quite a small machine, the kind with a transparent bulbous cabin at the front and room for just two or three people sitting side by side. It flew over the buildings, and whoever was in it must have been greatly interested in what was below, for it made a wide turn and came back to make another run over the same area.

'Somebody seems to be taking a close look at what's down there,' Brady remarked. 'I wonder who they are.'

'Could be someone doing a bit of aerial photography,' Linda said. 'They're low enough.'

'And that might not please the people on the ground. They seem to be the sort who value their privacy and would resent being spied on. From the ground or the air.'

'You're right about that,' Garfield said. 'Which just goes to prove they could have some valuable secrets.'

The helicopter had completed its second run, but it was still not going far away. It made another turn and came in again at a slightly different angle. And it was certainly attracting attention on the ground; even with the naked eye it was possible to see a lot of movement down there, though the figures were made small by the distance. Brady was put in mind of a nest of ants that had been disturbed.

'Oh, oh!' Garfield exclaimed. 'This looks like real trouble.' He was using the binoculars again.

'What are they doing?' Brady asked.

'They're bringing out the artillery. Here, you have a look.'

Brady took the glasses from him and focused them on the compound. And immediately he could see what Garfield had meant. There were more men down there now, and some of them had rifles or submachine-guns.

'Let me see,' Linda said.

Brady handed her the glasses and she had a look.

'Trouble is right,' she said. 'Let's just hope that chopper doesn't come back.'

But it had made another turn and was already on its way for a fourth pass over the compound. They could hear the clatter of its rotor blades growing ever louder. And then they saw it again, flying even lower than before.

'Now for it,' Brady said.

Suddenly the men on the ground opened fire with every weapon they had. The helicopter had come within range and it presented so large a target that it would have been almost impossible to miss. The pilot, becoming aware of the danger, tried to gain more altitude and veer away to the right. But it was far too late; the damage had been done. The helicopter cleared the compound and flew on; but there were flames coming from it. Even so it continued on its way for maybe 300 yards before dropping out of sight beyond a low ridge.

There was an explosion then, and a column of flame and

smoke rose from the spot where the machine had crashed to earth. Of the wreckage nothing could be seen by the watchers on the hill.

For a few moments all three were silent, shocked by what they had just seen. Then Brady said;

'Something tells me those people down there are pretty sensitive about having their pictures taken without permission. They get really worked up over it.'

'And that,' Linda said, 'can mean only one thing. They've got something to hide.'

'Too true. And another thing that occurs to me is that this would not be the best of times to go paying a call on them. They're far too handy with the armament.'

Even she was not prepared to argue with him on this point. And Garfield was saying nothing; he just looked unhappy.

'So what now?' Brady said. 'Do we just get to hell out? If anyone down there were to spot us we could be sitting ducks. And maybe dead ones.'

But Linda seemed unwilling to cut and run just yet. 'Let's wait and see what they do now. I'm interested.'

'OK then, if you insist. But keep your head down.'

They did not have long to wait for developments. A few minutes later two motor vehicles could be seen in the compound moving towards the gate. The first of these was of the Land-Rover type, and following it was a pick-up truck. The gate was opened to let them through, and they turned to the left and drove along the road until they came level with the corner of the perimeter fence, where it made a right-angle turn. A small distance beyond this point they left the road and drove away towards the place where the helicopter had come down, bumping and bouncing over the rough ground but making steady progress.

'Going to see what's left,' Brady said. 'I doubt whether there'll be any survivors.'

'And maybe shoot them if there are,' Linda suggested. And then: 'Now look at that.'

What she was indicating was a mechanical digger painted a bright yellow that was just leaving the compound and following on behind the other two vehicles.

Brady looked at it and a thought came into his head, a dark suspicion regarding what was afoot. For of what use would a mechanical digger be if not to dig? And what would it be going to dig but a grave? A grave large enough to accommodate the wreckage of the helicopter and the men who had been in it.

'The bastards are going to bury the evidence.'

'I think you're right,' Linda said. She spoke calmly, without emotion, as if this were something she would have expected and which was not in the least surprising. 'It just goes to show that they'll take any measures, however drastic, to prevent anyone from prying into their secrets. Which can only mean that those secrets are very important indeed. Just what in hell is going on in that place down there?'

'I'm not sure I really want to know,' Brady said.

'But you must want to. Have you no curiosity?'

'Not in this instance, I seem to remember that's what led to the death of the cat.'

The car, the truck and the digger were all out of sight now, and though smoke was still rising from the scene of the crash, it had thinned appreciably.

'This, I think,' Brady said, 'might be a good time to leave. That's if you aren't proposing to drive over there and see what the digger is doing.'

Even Miss Manning's curiosity did not push her quite as far
as that.

'OK,' she said. 'Let's go.'

Brady started to breathe more easily when the Shogun had put
a few miles behind it on the way back to Acapurno. What they
had witnessed that morning had given him no urge to proceed
further with this operation into which Linda Manning had
inveigled him. It was looking less and less free from all danger
to life and limb, and his dearest wish was to abandon it and
head for home. Unfortunately he feared that dear Linda would
not see eye to eye with him in this respect.

And she did not.

'Are you crazy?' she said when he put the suggestion to her.
'Or just plain craven.'

'Crazy, no. Craven, maybe. Cautious and prudent, certainly.'

'Well anyway, we can't turn back now. What would I tell our
people in London?'

'For one thing, they're not my people; I repudiate the idea
that they are. And for another, you could just tell them they
misled us.'

'In what way were we misled?'

'That man Forder said there'd be no risk. It seems to me now
that there's one hell of a risk. Wouldn't you agree?'

'Life's full of risks; they're a part of our existence. You can't
avoid them. You just have to carry on regardless.'

'And that's what you mean to do?'

'Of course.'

Brady sighed. He could see that there was no point in trying
to budge her on this. She had made up her mind that was that.
She would not be moved.

They came to the junction of the access road and the main one and headed back the way they had come earlier in the day. There was still not much traffic, but even at that it was more than they had encountered on the other stretch, either coming or going. It appeared that there was not a great deal of freight moving back and forth between the establishment within the wire perimeter fence and Acapurno and points beyond.

'I don't know whether you noticed, Linda,' Brady remarked, 'that some of those guys back there, those with the guns especially, had very dark skins and black hair. You could see this pretty clearly through the binocs.'

'What of it? A lot of Paraguayans look like that.'

'And yet to me they didn't look quite like Paraguayans.'

'They weren't,' Garfield said. 'They were Arabs.'

Linda sat up and took notice. 'Arabs! Are you sure?'

'Well, I know there are Arabs working there. Carlos told me. They're the ones who do the technical work, so he said. Guys like him, they just do the manual stuff. They have no idea what goes on in the laboratories and workshops and suchlike.'

'And yet he was going to get secret information that would be worth buying?'

'Yes. He reckoned he knew where that sort of thing was stored away. Plans, blueprints, formulae, all the low-down on what was going on. He promised he would get it for me.'

'And you believed him?'

'Why, yes. He seemed honest.'

'Honest! Ha! That's a good one. And now he's disappeared?'

'So it seems. I made inquiries yesterday, but it was no go. Couldn't get a clue.'

'You made inquiries? Where?'

'At the entrance gate to the compound. That was where I'd been yesterday. They wouldn't let me past the gate and they said they'd never heard of anyone named Carlos.'

'You were taking a risk, weren't you? Going there openly like that. They know you now.'

'I suppose so,' Garfield said. And he seemed unhappy about it. 'But I was getting desperate. I talked to the guard on the gate first. He knew nothing, but he got on the phone and one of the Arabs came out and talked to me. He wanted to know why I was interested in this Carlos character, and he seemed pretty suspicious.'

'I'm not surprised. Did you tell him who you were?'

'No. But I'm afraid now that they may have got on to Carlos and prised the information out of him.'

Brady could understand now why Garfield was so scared. People who would shoot down a helicopter would not think twice about eliminating a spy like Carlos and then maybe the man he had been in touch with on the outside: none other than Harold Garfield, as ever was.

'I think,' Linda said, 'we'd better have some more discussion about this when we get back to your place. Meanwhile, I'll have to do a bit of serious thinking. This business isn't going quite according to plan, is it?'

And that, Brady reflected, was the understatement of the year. It was all to have been so simple, and now look: complication on complication and people getting themselves killed and whatever. Really, when you came to think about it, it was just like the old days.

And he was afraid it could get worse.

Chapter Thirteen

THE BRIGHT SIDE

It was one o'clock when they arrived back at the caravan. They had not eaten since breakfast, but there were more important matters on their minds than the question of lunch. Garfield made coffee and fished out a packet of biscuits, and they made a meal of them.

'And now, Harold old man,' Linda said, 'let's have it all. Straight from the horse's mouth, as the saying is.'

'What do you want to know?'

'Everything. For a start, how did you come to discover that place with the ring fence and the guard on the gate?'

'I was told about it.'

'So you were told about it. By whom?'

Garfield squirmed a little, as though reluctant to admit who his informant had been. But, seeing no way out of it, he said: 'Pedro.'

'Ruiz! How did he get to hear of it?'

'Oh, there were rumours going around in Asunción and he used to keep his ear to the ground. There was nothing definite, of course, but it seemed odd, this place out in the wilds. It was a mystery.'

'So he passed on what he had heard to you.'

'Yes. He thought I might be interested.'

'And of course you were.'

'Yes. That was when I decided to come out to this place. Acapurno's the nearest town, you see. So it seemed a good idea to make it my base. Then I started making inquiries, and I found quite a few people who had heard about this mysterious establishment, but no one could tell me exactly where it was. None of them had actually seen it and they didn't seem to be particularly interested. It was all very frustrating.'

'I can imagine,' Linda said. 'So what then?'

'I began to wonder whether I was just wasting my time, because I appeared to be getting nowhere, and there was no certainty that in the end there would be anything for me to send back to Adsum. I was half inclined to pack it in and return to Asunción, where I had one or two leads to other businesses that might have been worth following up.'

'Why didn't you?'

'Oh, I don't know. I suppose I was just hooked on this thing. Like I said, it was a mystery and I was intrigued. And then I had a piece of luck: this man Carlos turned up. It was in a bar. I'd been pointed out to him apparently, and he'd been told I was asking questions about this factory or whatever it was out in the wilderness. Well, we got to talking and it turned out he actually worked in the place and he was in town for a spot of relaxation. He'd had a few drinks and I bought him more and his tongue began to wag. He told me where the place was and what it was like and what he did there.'

'And what was that?'

'Oh, nothing important. Shifting stuff around, sweeping up and that sort of thing. Unskilled labour.'

'Did you ask him what was produced there?'

'Yes, of course. And he said there was nothing.'

'Nothing?'

'Yes. He said lorries would come in with supplies of this and that, but they just went away empty. There'd be fuel tankers too, to supply the electricity generators and so on.'

'So it's not a factory?'

'Apparently not. My guess is it's some kind of research establishment, and Carlos himself hinted at that.'

'So then you asked him if he could get you some information regarding this research?'

'Not at once. I had to work up to it. We had other meetings from time to time.'

'How did he get to town?'

'On a motor-bike.'

'So no restrictions were placed on his movements?'

'Seems not. I suppose as he was only a sort of odd-job man it was not imagined he could give any secrets away. After all, the lorry drivers came and went. It was not as if the existence of the establishment was a secret; it was only what went on inside those buildings that was hush-hush.'

'The work that the Arabs do?'

'They and a number of non-Arabs; scientists, technicians and the like, who all keep themselves apart from the manual workers like Carlos. They live in better quarters and some of them have families there. There's a gymnasium and indoor swimming pool and plenty of other facilities for them. Seems like it's quite a feudal set-up.'

'Did Carlos know about the guns?'

'He didn't say. He told me about the guard on the gate and that no unauthorized visitors were allowed inside the fence.'

'So finally you asked him if he could get you some information regarding what was really going on there?'

'Yes. He'd already hinted that he might be able to get secret papers for me. At a price.'

'And of course you took him up on that.'

'Yes.'

'So that was when you decided to jump the gun and get in touch with Adsum? Before the thing was in the bag or you even knew what it would be.'

Garfield did some more of the squirming and tried to justify his action. 'I felt sure he would come up with the goods. He seemed so confident. And anything that was worth guarding so carefully was bound to be hot property, wasn't it?'

'But all this must have been weeks ago. And you've seen nothing of him since?'

'Not a sign. He was supposed to bring the material to me here. But he hasn't turned up. I've been worried out of my mind.'

'And with reason, I should imagine,' Linda said. 'One can only assume that he was caught red-handed and dealt with accordingly.'

'And judging by what we've seen,' Brady added, 'they're not likely to have handled him with kid gloves. Frankly, Harold, I don't think you're ever going to see friend Carlos again.'

It was evident that Garfield had already come to this conclusion himself, and he was not liking it one little bit. No doubt at first he had had no suspicion that this game he had become involved in would turn out to be no game at all but a very lethal operation. Perhaps now he would have very much liked to walk away from it but could see no easy way of doing so. That his mind was working on these lines was evidenced by his next words.

'I don't see that there's anything more we can do now. It's been a total washout. I'm sorry.'

'So you should be,' Linda said. 'This has cost Adsum quite a lot of money and they're not going to be at all happy about that. You do see, don't you?'

'Well, yes, but—'

'Still, all may not be lost. What I suggest is that we all sleep on this and tomorrow morning we'll have another conference and see whether we can come up with something. Right?'

Brady's personal opinion was that this was not such a great idea. He could see no way now that they were going to get any secret documents out of that well-guarded establishment in the wilds, and he felt that the only sensible course was to call it a day and head for England, home and beauty. But knowing Miss Manning as well as he did, he was quite sure that she would not be prepared to give in quite so easily. He could see that Garfield was not exactly eager to have that discussion in the morning either. His acceptance of the suggestion was certainly rather lacking in enthusiasm.

'Well, if you really think so.'

'I do,' she said.

And that was that.

Rex Petersen put in an appearance when they were having an evening meal at the inn.

'You folks had a good day?' he asked.

'So-so,' Linda said.

Petersen laughed. 'Only so-so? Nothing exciting to make things interesting?'

Brady thought of telling him about the shot-down helicopter, because that was surely exciting and interesting enough for anyone's taste. But then he thought better of it, since he was pretty certain that Linda would not approve. It was evident that Petersen had heard nothing about it; which was not really surprising, seeing that the only outside witnesses of the incident were Linda and Garfield and himself; while those who had done the shooting had been quick to cover all traces of the tragic event.

He supposed the proper course to take would be to go to the local police and report the incident; leaving it to them to go out and investigate. But that seemed not even to have occurred to either Linda or Garfield, and he himself was none too keen on getting involved with the Paraguayan lawmen, so he let it go.

'And what have you been doing?' Linda asked. 'Taking a lot of splendid pictures?'

'I've done one or two.'

'When are you planning to move on?'

'Haven't decided yet. I'll maybe stick around for a while longer. And you?'

'Oh, we'll stick around too. For the present.'

Brady had a feeling that Petersen's interest in their movements might be rather more than casual, though he could see no good reason why it should have been. In the easygoing way of Americans he had immediately taken to addressing them by their first names and had invited them to call him Rex. It was as if they were old friends, though in fact they had as yet spent scarcely more than an hour in each others' company.

And then Petersen said quite casually, almost as though he were talking to himself: 'I wonder what does go on behind that wire fence. I'd sure like to know.'

It caught both Linda and Brady off balance, and neither of them said anything for a moment or two. Brady was aware that

Petersen was watching them closely, his pale blue eyes slightly narrowed; most certainly aware of their reaction and waiting for a reponse to his remark.

Then Linda said softly: 'What fence would that be?'

'Why,' Petersen said, 'the one surrounding a lot of buildings and whatnot way out to the north of town. You aren't going to tell me you haven't seen it.'

'Why should we have seen it?' Brady asked.

Then Petersen laughed softly and said: 'OK, let it go. But brother, you don't kid me. You're not here for the sake of your health any more than I am. Am I right or am I not?'

Neither Linda nor Brady said anything. They just looked at him in silence.

And after that he started talking about something entirely different and said never another word about that place with the wire fence round it, away to the north.

'Who is he?' Linda said later, when they were alone together. 'And more to the point, what is he and what is he doing here?'

'So you don't believe he's a photographer working on a project for the *National Geographic*?'

'I never did fully believe that tale. It seemed just too unlikely to my way of thinking.'

'As our tale did to him apparently. Well, one thing is certain: he knows about that place we visited this morning. But he couldn't have been around at the time. I'd say he doesn't know a thing about the chopper being shot down.'

'That's true. And now I have a feeling that it's something he'd be very interested indeed to hear about.'

'It crossed my mind to tell him.'

'Why didn't you?'

'Oh, I had this odd feeling that you might not have altogether approved of it.'

'And of course, Steve darling, you never do anything that doesn't meet with my approval, do you?'

'I try not to.'

'Not always with complete success. Anyway, I think in this case it might be as well not to confide too much in our Mr Petersen until we know him rather better.'

'You're probably right.'

'And tomorrow we'll pay another call on Garfield.'

Brady sighed. 'I suppose so.' He himself would have been well contented if he were never to see Garfield again as long as he lived; but in this bad old world you just had to resign yourself to doing a whole raft of things you would much rather not do. And for him meeting dear old Harold again was one of them.

'Cheer up,' Linda said. 'Try to look on the bright side.'

And she kissed him; possibly to demonstrate that there was a bright side. Which was nice. But he would still have been happier if they had been planning to leave for Asunción in the morning.

Chapter Fourteen

INTERROGATION

It was around nine o'clock in the morning when they arrived once again at Garfield's temporary home. There were people up and about in the hollow, some of them gathered in groups, apparently engaged in animated discussion. They all fell silent and stared at Linda and Brady as they walked past on their way to the caravan. The van-dwellers had never shown much interest in them before, and Brady wondered why they should do so on this occasion. But it did not bother him.

The Shogun was standing where it had been when they got out of it the previous afternoon, so it seemed probable that Garfield had not used it again. Maybe he had stayed in the van or had even gone for a walk, although he had not given the impression of being a man who did much walking for the sake of his health. So maybe he had, after they left him, drunk himself into a stupor in an attempt to forget his worries and had then gone to sleep. He might even be still sleeping, for the curtains were drawn across the windows.

'I don't believe he's up yet,' Linda said. 'He's a lazy devil.'

She mounted the steps and rapped on the door. There was no

answer. Impatiently she tried the handle and the door opened easily; it had not been locked. She went inside, followed closely by Brady.

'Oh, my God!' she said.

Garfield was there, but he was not asleep, except in the sense that death is the long sleep from which there is no awakening. He was in pyjamas and he was lying on one of the settees with a blanket half covering him. He was on his back with his head resting on a pillow, and his eyes were open and staring glassily at nothing in particular. He had been killed very neatly with a bullet to the brain. The small hole where it had gone in was visible in the centre of his forehead, and it was possibly buried in the pillow if one cared to look. There was very little blood to be seen.

'Well, well, well!' Brady said. 'Seems he had good reason to be scared. I wonder when they did this to him.'

'Does it matter?' Linda said. 'Sometime in the night, no doubt. Shut the door. We've got to do some thinking. This rather complicates things.'

As always, she was cool. No panicking for Miss Manning.

Brady closed the door. It cut off some of the light, and now they had only what was leaking through the curtains. But these were made of flimsy material and the sun was shining outside, so it was enough.

'The question that arises,' Linda said, 'is this. What is the best course of action for us to take now that this has happened?'

'Oughtn't we to go to the police?'

She gave him a withering look. 'Do you really want to get involved with them?'

He could see that she was not in favour of this move, and on the whole he tended to agree with her.

'So what do we do? Just walk away and leave him like this? We've been seen coming to the caravan, remember.'

'Yes,' she admitted, 'that is awkward.'

'It's odd the door not being locked. Do you think he forgot to lock it?'

'Maybe. Or maybe they knocked and he let them in.'

'Would he have done that? And besides he was lying on the bed when they shot him.'

'So maybe they made him lie down before doing it. Or maybe the lock on the door is broken. It's all immaterial anyway.'

'What puzzles me about old Harold,' Brady said, 'is how he ever got into this game and how he managed to make a living as Adsum's man in Paraguay. Surely there couldn't have been that much opportunity for him here.'

'You're right,' Linda said. 'My understanding is that it was just a sideline with him while he went about his other business. He had several irons in the fire, so it seems; none of them getting very hot, but enough for him to manage on. He appears for one thing to have been a kind of freelance sales rep for a number of small British exporting firms which did a little business in Paraguay. This present Adsum job was probably looking to be the biggest thing he'd handled. You heard him say he was hooked on it. Maybe he thought it was his big break.'

'And in the end it just came to this – a bullet in the noggin.'

'Well, that's how it goes.'

'There's another thing I don't understand. Why did Garfield have to use Ruiz as a go-between? Why couldn't he have just given Adsum this address in Acapurno?'

'Perhaps because it wasn't permanent. He said he'd only recently moved here. Or maybe he'd got this idea into his head that he was some kind of secret agent and had to go through all the tricks. It could have been a role he was playing, a sort of Walter Mitty thing.'

'And in the end he found himself out of his depth and discovered what a deadly game it was.'

'Exactly.'

They were both silent for a moment. Then Brady said: 'You've been holding out on me again.'

'In what way?'

'You knew all about friend Harold before we left England; what he did for a living and so on. Yet you gave me the impression that until you opened that envelope we picked up at Ruiz's place you'd never heard his name.'

'I hadn't. Adsum never told me his name. He was just our man in the field. That's their way, you see. Secrecy, secrecy, secrecy. The left hand mustn't know what the right hand is doing.'

'And how that really takes me back to former days.'

They were still standing there, undecided what their next move ought to be, when they heard the sound of a car pulling up outside. A moment later the door of the caravan burst open and a burly man in uniform came in, followed closely by another. Both men were armed with pistols, and it took no great powers of deduction to conclude that they were policemen. The chevrons on the sleeve of the burly one appeared to indicate his rank, possibly that of sergeant.

It was an awkward situation, to say the least. Here they were in a caravan with a dead man who had all too obviously been shot in the head. What could have looked more suspicious?

It was not difficult to figure out why the police had arrived at that moment. Evidently someone else had discovered Garfield's body before they had; and that someone had departed hotfoot to inform the local constabulary. It had been the misfortune of Linda Manning and Stephen Brady to turn up for their appointment with Garfield in the interval between the departure of the one and the arrival of the others.

As if to add further evidence that this had indeed been the sequence of events, another person had appeared in the doorway. This was an unattractive male of indeterminate age and hangdog aspect. He was saying something that Brady failed to catch and pointing at the body on the settee, and it seemed more than likely that he was the one who had paid a visit to the caravan for some purpose or other, had spotted the dead occupant and carried the news to the forces of law and order.

Brady was to recall what ensued as one of the less pleasant episodes in a life that had certainly had its bad moments; not to say minutes, hours, days and even weeks. To anyone with a grain of commonsense it should have been obvious that he and Linda were innocent parties in this piece of gruesome business; for the dead body had been discovered before they had arrived at the caravan; and if they had done the killing, why on earth would they have returned to the scene of the crime so shortly afterwards? It would have been sheer madness.

But this argument appeared to cut no ice with the policemen. Perhaps to them it seemed entirely possible that the two of them were mad. After all, were they not foreigners? And of foreigners, gringos moreover, one could expect anything. The upshot of it was that they were arrested on suspicion and taken, handcuffed, to the Acapurno police station.

This was a plain brick building near the centre of the town. Here they were conducted to separate offices for interrogation, and Brady found himself in a stuffy little room with a desk and some filing cabinets and a couple of hard wooden chairs, a considerable clutter of official-looking papers and a board with notices of various kinds pinned to it, some yellow with age. He was released from the handcuffs and searched, and his passport was taken from him and examined by a large fat man in a short-sleeved shirt with sweat stains under the armpits, whose rank was not apparent. This man was seated behind the desk, but Brady was not invited to sit down.

'So,' the fat man said, wheezing like an inflated bladder with a puncture, 'you are British.' He made it sound like an accusation, as though this in itself constituted a misdemeanour.

Brady admitted that he was indeed British.

'And what is the purpose of your visit to Acapurno?'

'Recreation.'

'You are travelling for pleasure?'

'Yes.'

'And the woman is your wife?'

'No.'

'And in Acapurno where are you staying?'

'In an inn near the plaza. The innkeeper's name is Cortés. We have a room.'

'Just one room.'

'Yes.'

'Ah!'

Brady wondered whether this would count against him. Was the fat officer something of a puritan, even if he did not look like one? Appearances could be deceptive, and there was no telling what the man's moral code might be.

The fact of the matter was that Brady found himself in somewhat of a quandary. Being separated from Linda, he had no means of telling what answers she was giving to questions put to her. They might not match his; so he had to be wary and as non-committal as possible.

'Why did you shoot the man Garfield?' the man in the sweaty shirt asked; snapping out the question suddenly, as if to catch the prisoner off guard.

'I did not shoot him,' Brady said.

'So it was the woman who did it?'

'No. She did not shoot him either. He was already dead when we got to the caravan.'

'Why did you go there?'

'We had an appointment to meet Mr Garfield at nine o'clock.'

'When did you make this appointment you say you had?'

'When we left him yesterday afternoon.'

'So you were with him yesterday?'

'Yes.'

'Was Mr Garfield a friend of yours?'

'Not of mine, no.'

'But a friend of Miss Manning?'

'You will have to ask her that.'

'She did not tell you?'

'She doesn't tell me everything. I'm just a travelling companion.'

'Who sleeps with the lady?'

Brady did not answer that one. He could see that the man did not believe him. This was not surprising; the story was about as unbelievable as you could get. The interrogation went on for a while longer, and then he was taken out of the office and locked in a cell. It was down a short flight of steps and the only light that came in was from a small window well above head level in one wall. It was a dank and chilly place, with a hard bunk and a couple of coarse grey blankets which one of the police officers brought. In these dismal quarters he was destined to spend the rest of the day and the night.

He was to learn later that Linda's interrogation had been similar to his own, though in her case there had been the complication of the gun. They had searched her shoulder bag and inevitably had found the Smith & Wesson self-loading pistol. She said they were quite excited about this until they examined it more closely and could see that it had not been fired recently, and perhaps never had been, except maybe for testing. It was certainly not the weapon that had killed Harold Garfield; which was a great disappointment to them.

As to the questions, she had done her best to stonewall. She had told them that she knew very little about Garfield. A friend in England who knew she was travelling to Paraguay had given her his name and address and had suggested she should visit him if she were ever in the area. This she had done, taking Brady with her for company. By luck this fitted in fairly well with Brady's own story; but whether or not it was believed was quite another matter. It certainly did not save her from also spending some time in a cell.

The sanitary arrangements in his accommodation were primitive, but the food was rather better than might have been expected. Brady supposed one had to be thankful for small mercies.

He spent most of the night thinking about his future and hoping he had one.

Chapter Fifteen

MAN IN GREY

They were taken from their cells at about eleven o'clock the next morning and were both conducted to the room where Miss Manning had been interrogated. This was somewhat larger than that in which the man in the sweaty shirt had questioned Brady, but it was just as cluttered.

The first thing he noticed when he entered was that there was a man he had never seen before standing with his back to the door and staring out of a window which appeared to provide a view of nothing more interesting than a yard with a stunted tree in the centre of it. Possibly the man liked stunted trees.

When he turned it was possible to see that he had a lean hatchet face, black hair slicked back from the somewhat bulging forehead, a thin-lipped mouth and eyes that somehow gave the impression of being ice-cold. He was tall and slightly stooping, perhaps between forty-five and fifty years of age, and dressed in an immaculate pale-grey suit.

Without preamble he apologized for the wrongful arrest which had led to Miss Manning and Mr Brady spending the night in captivity.

'It was,' he said, 'a mistaken and over-zealous act on the part of the Acapurno police, which I greatly deplore.'

Those members of the Acapurno police force who were present looked distinctly uncomfortable and red-faced at this, but they said nothing. They seemed to be thoroughly cowed by the man in the grey suit.

'I hope,' the man said, 'you will choose to overlook this unfortunate incident and will not regard it as typical of the way we normally treat overseas visitors to our country.'

'I should certainly hope not,' Linda said. 'It was not at all pleasant. The cells here are disgusting.'

Brady said nothing.

'Your possessions will of course be returned to you and a car will be provided to take you to your hotel or anywhere else you may wish to go.'

The man in grey was so eager to be obliging that Brady wondered whether he might offer some compensation for the inconvenience that had been inflicted on the strangers within the gates. But he did not go as far as that. He added a few more words of apology, and then the interview came to an end. He had told them neither his name nor his rank, but he obviously had authority and was well able to cow the keepers of the law in Acapurno. It seemed probable that there had been telephone contact with the authorities in Asunción and he had speedily been sent out to deal with the situation. Possibly the decision had been his own.

They were driven back to the inn in a police car with a sullen police officer at the wheel. Linda had her shoulder bag, and in it was the pistol which had been so eagerly seized the previous day. It was no longer regarded as evidence in the murder inquiry. And maybe the inquiry itself had been abandoned after the visit of the man in grey. Strange things seemed to be happening.

Brady wondered how they would be received by the landlord and his wife. They had not returned from the morning outing on the previous day, and it was probably common knowledge that they had been arrested, since in a town the size of Acapurno such matters had a way of quickly becoming common knowledge. So maybe mine host would exhibit some coldness or even hostility towards his guests, knowing that they had spent the night in cells. Possibly he would even tell them that they were no longer welcome under his roof.

Nothing could have been further from the truth. In the event they were greeted with more warmth than had ever been previously shown to them. It seemed that their recent contretemps with the local constabulary, far from alienating them from the landlord and his wife, had quite endeared them, not only to these good people, but to all the regular clientele of the inn. Obviously the police were not held in high esteem by the general public, or at least not by that part of it which patronized that particular house. And so Linda and Brady, simply by having been arrested and thrown into the cells, had achieved almost heroic status in the eyes of those around them.

'Those police,' the landlord said, and he looked as though he would have liked to spit if there had been any convenient receptacle to receive the spittle. 'Animals, swine, donkeys! They are not worth that.' And he snapped his fingers. 'You were ill-treated?'

'It could have been worse,' Brady said. 'Though of course we would have preferred to sleep here.'

'You will tonight,' his wife said. 'With a good supper inside you. I will see to that.'

Even the slatternly girl added her tribute by gazing at Brady with adoration in her eyes. It was all quite embarrassing.

As soon as they were in their room he said: 'Can we go home now?'

'Is that what you want?'

'You bet it is. And the way I see it, there's nothing to keep us here any longer. We're not going to get anything from Garfield now, and I don't think it was ever likely that we would. This whole operation has been a damp squib from start to finish and there's no point in hanging on, because when it comes to the crunch Acapurno is not exactly a holiday resort on the Thomas Cook circuit. And neither is Asunción in my opinion.'

Linda made no reply to this; she seemed to be thinking of something else. Then she said: 'I wonder who the man in the grey suit was. I'd like to know.'

'Does it matter? He got us off the hook and that's the main thing, wouldn't you say?'

'So he must have authority. And another thing, why would he be so keen to do it? Are we that important?'

'Maybe we are. Maybe the people in Asunción, the people in charge of affairs, don't fancy having the complication of a couple of British tourists charged with murder. Bad for the holiday trade.'

'If there is any.'

'Well, can you think of a more probable reason?'

She said thoughtfully: 'Maybe I can. Suppose it has something to do with that other business.'

'What other business?'

'Why, the place we went to look at, of course. Suppose there are people in high places who don't want attention drawn to it, and so would like to put a lid on the Garfield murder and everything connected with it.'

'For what reason?'

'For the very good reason that they've got an interest in what goes on out there.'

'Now you're just guessing.'

'So what if I am? There's a mystery here and it bothers me. What I suggest is that we get ourselves cleaned up in what passes here for a bathroom and then go and see what's happened down at the caravan site during our absence in the lock-up.'

Brady groaned. 'Must we?'

'Yes,' Linda said, 'we must.'

And he knew then that they would not be going home just yet.

They bathed together in order to economize on the hot water. At least, that was what Linda said. Brady made no excuse.

Then they put on some clean clothes, and feeling that the lingering odour of the police cells had finally been washed away, they took a walk down to the hollow where the caravans were parked.

It seemed pretty quiet down there. No doubt the brief excitement of the previous morning had worn off and things were back to normal. The Shogun was gone, though the imprint of its tyres remained as mute testimony that it had once been there. The curtains were still drawn across the windows of the caravan, but it was pretty certain that Garfield's body was not inside. The police would have taken it away, and where it would end up was anybody's guess. Brady got the impression of something abandoned, the occupant departed, never to return. Would his ghost perhaps haunt the van?

'It's spooky,' he said.

'Nonsense,' Linda said. 'It's just an empty caravan.'

'Well, now we've seen it, let's go. You don't want to look inside, I suppose?'

'No, that won't be necessary. Nothing in there for us.'

Petersen was at the inn when they got back. He was propping up the bar, a glass of beer close at hand. He looked relaxed.

'Hey!' he said. 'What's this I hear about you two getting arrested on a murder rap?'

'If you heard it you don't need us to tell you,' Linda said.

'Guess that's so. Glad to see they let you go again.'

'It was all a mistake,' Brady said.

'Who was this guy Garfield who got killed? Friend of yours, was he?'

'Not really.'

'Way I heard it, you just happened to be with the cadaver when the cops moved in.'

'You seem to hear a lot,' Linda said.

'I keep my ear to the ground.'

'That's as good a way as any to get earache, so I've been told.'

Petersen laughed. 'Sure looks like you're having an interesting vacation.'

'Very interesting. You should try it yourself sometime. The inside of a police cell in this town is an architectural feature much to be admired.'

'I'll take your word for that. You leaving now?'

Linda shook her head. 'Not just yet.'

'We just can't tear ourselves away,' Brady said.

Petersen nodded. 'I know how it is.'

And Brady wondered whether he did. With a man like Petersen you could not be sure. You could not be sure at all.

Chapter Sixteen

NIGHT DRIVE

It was Linda who drove. Brady offered to, but she said she would do it. And maybe that was as it should have been, because he had not wanted to go at all; he had argued with her and said there was no sense in it; but she had been adamant.

'If you don't want to come, you don't have to. I'll go by myself.'

And of course when she said that he knew there was no way he, Stephen Brady, could pull out. He had to go with her.

They had called at the only garage in the town for petrol earlier in the day, and the Beetle had a full tank. Now, as they set out, the light was fading and it would soon be dark. Fortunately, it appeared that the car's lighting system was in good order. Brady just hoped it would not go on the blink when they were miles from town; but sod's law told him that it would.

If the road out to the north of Acapurno had been a fairly dismal highway in daylight, it was far worse in the dark. The headlights' beams exaggerated the potholes and ruts, and on either side the bleak landscape merged into the darkness, with scarcely a lighted window to show that life existed in that barren wasteland. Only occasionally would the lamps of an approaching car or lorry indicate that there was other traffic on the road and sometimes force Linda to take the Beetle off to the side, where the going was rougher and more hazardous than in the middle.

'I'm really enjoying this,' Brady said. 'There's nothing like a nice excursion out into the countryside, is there? Especially at night.'

The sarcasm was wasted on Linda. She just said: 'Stop moaning. You haven't done much yet to earn your money, so what have you got to complain about?'

'I haven't seen a lot of that money yet. And I wouldn't be surprised if when it comes to the point Adsum refuse to fork out, because as I see it the entire operation has been little better than a bloody shambles from start to finish. And I do mean bloody.'

'It isn't finished yet. Don't be so defeatist.'

'I'm not defeatist; I'm just being realistic. What can you hope to achieve by this nocturnal expedition into the wilderness? I hope you're not proposing to drive up to the gate and demand to be allowed inside for a tour around the establishment.'

'Now you're being stupid.'

'Well, what are you going to do?'

'We'll see when we get there.'

He decided to leave it at that. What was the use of arguing? She would have her way, come what might.

They almost missed the fork where the newer road branched off to the left. It was Brady who noticed it as they went by.

'There!' he shouted. 'There it is. The other road.'

She had driven past, but she stopped the car and backed it to the junction and got it on to the right track.

'You're lucky to have me with you,' Brady said. 'You could have gone on for miles. I have my uses after all.'

'Have I ever said you didn't?'

'Maybe not. But sometimes I get the impression.'

'Never believe it, Steve,' she said. 'We're a team, you and I. Always have been. This is an old pals act, isn't it?'

'You really mean that?'

'Sure I do. There's never been anyone like you in my life. Never.'

It pleased him to hear her say this. It gave him a certain glow in the region where he supposed his heart was. It was just a pity that being in this team so often had a way of getting him into sticky situations. But that, of course, was the nature of it.

Now that they were on the branch road the going was somewhat less rough and there was no traffic at all coming to meet them. Brady tried to pick out landmarks that might help him to judge how close they were getting to their destination, but it was difficult; there was such a lack of any conspicuous objects in that almost featureless landscape, to which now was added the cloak of darkness.

It was the upward slope that eventually gave them warning. There had been other inclines along the way, both up and down, but this was noticeably steeper than any of the others.

'I think we're nearly there,' Linda said.

She stopped the car and switched off the headlights; and then they could see a glow ahead that had its origin beyond the summit of the little hill. There was only one possible source of this light; it had to be the fenced-in establishment they had seen two days ago.

'That's it,' Brady said. 'No doubt about it.'

Linda put the Beetle into reverse and backed it down the

slope until they came to what she judged to be somewhere near the place where Garfield had taken the Shogun into the shelter of the scrub. There she took the Beetle off the road but did not drive it so deeply into cover as Garfield had done with the other vehicle. It had been broad daylight then; now there was the darkness to hide them.

She switched off the lights and the ignition, and they sat for a few minutes in the silence, just waiting, as though each were hesitating to make the next move. Brady wondered whether his companion was experiencing a similar feeling to his own: the sense that in the car was a kind of safety that would be abandoned immediately they stepped outside. Opening a door would take an effort of will, for it would entail the abandonment of that refuge, a venture into the unknown.

'We could still turn around and drive away,' he said.

As he might have guessed, the very suggestion was enough to galvanize her. She would not have come this far only to abandon the project, to turn tail and run for home.

'Don't be ridiculous,' she said. 'Though if you're having cold feet you can stay in the car. I'll go on my own.'

Once again of course she had really given him no choice. He had to go with her. He gave a sigh.

'All right. Let's get on with it.'

They both got out, Linda taking her shoulder bag with her, in which Brady knew was the gun and a small torch. It was not quite so impenetrably dark as he had imagined it would be. The scrub was a block of deeper blackness, but there was the glow from the compound showing above the rise. In the present conditions they were able to approach with less caution than they had exercised on the previous visit. They got themselves on to the road and advanced up it to a point from which they could gaze down on the fencing and the buildings and the parked vehicles. There were lights in various places, but they could observe no one moving around. As might have been expected, the entrance gate was closed and no doubt locked, but there was no gatekeeper to be seen, though there might have been one or more in the small building at the side.

'So what now?' Brady asked. 'We've seen the place by lamp-light, but what does that tell us that we didn't know before?'

'Nothing. But don't be impatient. We haven't finished yet,' Linda said.

He was afraid of that. She had come to make an investigation, a reconnoitre of the place, and she would not think of leaving until she had done so.

'Let's go this way,' she said. And she moved off to the right of the road, with Brady following willy-nilly close behind.

The ground underfoot was rough and tussocky, but there was enough firmness in it to make walking easy enough. The chief hazard was tripping on one of the tussocks and falling, since it was impossible to see clearly what one was treading on. They were keeping well away from the fence so that the lights from the compound would not reveal their presence to anyone inside. Only a searchlight aimed in their direction would have picked them out from the darkness, and so they were able to progress unobserved on a line parallel with but not too close to the wire barrier on their left. For what purpose Linda was making this manoeuvre Brady failed to understand, but he supposed she had something in mind.

About a hundred yards on they came to an obstacle. This was another of those clumps of scrub that constituted one of the few features of the area. It grew quite close up to the fence at that point and was maybe fifty yards wide.

'We'll have to make a detour,' Linda said. 'I don't fancy pushing through this lot.'

So they made the detour and reached the other side of the obstacle. And that was when Brady saw the first flicker of lightning in the distance ahead, followed some seconds later by a low rumble of thunder.

'Oh, oh!' he said. 'Now there's a storm brewing. That's all we need.'

'It's a long way off. May never reach us.'

'So you're going to press on regardless?'

'Certainly. What did you think?'

'I thought you would,' Brady said.

They left the patch of scrub behind and soon after this they came level with the corner of the perimeter fence. There they came to a halt. Inside the fence at this point they could see the smaller buildings which Garfield had told them were living-quarters. There were lights visible in several windows.

'Now where do we go from here?' Brady asked.

'I'd like to see where that helicopter came down.'

'Why?'

'As a matter of interest.'

'And how do you propose finding it in the dark?'

'It can't be far. If we just go straight on we're bound to come to it.'

'Well, if you must.'

It proved less difficult than he had expected. They came to where the ground dropped away fairly steeply to a hollow, and here, with the aid of Linda's torch, they found charred grass and freshly dug earth. There were marks that had undoubtedly been made by the digger and smaller ones left by the wheels of the pick-up truck and the four-wheel drive vehicle. There was no sign of any bodies or the wreckage of the helicopter.

'They seem to have made a good job of it,' Linda said. 'Before long there'll be nothing to give a clue to what happened the other day.'

'Even if anyone came looking for a clue. Which is doubtful.'

There was another flicker of lightning and a rumble of thunder, rather closer now. A wind sprang up and died away again almost immediately. There seemed to Brady to be a dampness in the air.

'I think we really should go now.'

This time she made no argument, but turned and began to walk back the way they had come. They skirted the belt of scrub, and there she came to a halt.

'I've just had an idea.'

'What is it?' Brady asked. And he had more misgivings, because when she had an idea in a situation like this it usually turned out to be the prelude to another risky move.

'It occurred to me that if we were to make our way through this bit of a wood we'd be able to get quite close to the fence without being seen by anyone on the inside.'

He had to admit that it might be possible. 'But to what purpose?'

'To take a closer look, of course.'

'And you want to do that?'

'Well, naturally. Isn't that what we came for?'

'It's what you came for, I suppose. I just came along for the ride. And I've known better.'

'Come along then.'

It was tougher going than they might have imagined; the scrub seemed thicker here and Brady could feel thorns going into his flesh, branches slapping him in the face. There was no difficulty in keeping to the right line, since the glow from the lights on the other side of the fence showed through the screen. What was less pleasing was the fact that the thunderstorm was undoubtedly coming nearer. Another gust of wind brought with it heavy raindrops which pattered on the leaves.

Then they were at the wire and could see into the lighted compound. They were still looking in when they saw the dogs.

Chapter Seventeen

SHOT IN THE ARM

There were two of them, Dobermans, big, powerful, ugly brutes. They came running silently at first, but full of menace. They began to bark when they got near the fence and they leaped at it, growling and snarling, fangs bared and dripping saliva.

Involuntarily, Linda and Brady drew back, though it was obvious that the dogs could neither scale the fence nor break through it. They could only threaten.

'Charming pets,' Brady said. 'I'm glad we're out here and not in there. I never did fancy being a dog's dinner.'

There was another scud of rain. A lightning flash gave its brief, blinding light and was followed almost immediately by a tremendous crack of thunder. The storm had come up very quickly and was now overhead. This latest thunderclap, so close and ear-splitting, was too much for the dogs; they turned tail and fled.

Brady was glad to see them go, and he felt it was high time he and Linda were leaving too. The wisdom of making this move was emphasized by the appearance on the scene of a man with a gun. He must have heard the noise the dogs had been making and had come running to see what it was all about. He had apparently spotted them on the other side of the fence and he was not intimidated by the thunder as the animals had been. He ran towards them, shouting something that was lost in the increasing clamour of the wind.

This time it was Linda who said with some urgency: 'Come on. Let's go.'

She turned away from the fence and plunged into the cover of the thicket of scrub. Brady did not hesitate to follow, and as he did so he heard the crackle of a submachine-gun and knew what kind of weapon it was that the man on the other side of the fence was carrying. It was not the sort of knowledge that was calculated to add anything to his peace of mind, especially when he caught the sound of some of the bullets whipping into the bushes close at hand. The awareness of this threat to his life was sufficient incentive to press forward and ignore the thorns and brambles that were tearing at him and doing their damnedest to impede his progress. He noted that Linda too was making pretty good headway in spite of the unseen obstacles in the way, and she was a good two or three yards ahead of him when they finally reached open country. The man with the gun had already ceased firing.

'You OK, Linda?' he asked.

'Apart from scratches, yes.'

'That was a close call. With those boys in there it seems to be a case of shoot first and ask questions afterwards.'

'He may have been only trying to scare us.'

'If so, as far as I'm concerned he made a pretty good job of it. But do you really believe he was not aiming to wing us?'

'Frankly, I don't. They're obviously a sensitive bunch. Dogs and armed night-watchmen. What does that tell you?'

'That they don't like intruders.'

'And that they've got something to hide. Something very important. I'd like to know just what that is.'

'Personally,' Brady said, 'I can live quite happily without the knowledge. Especially if to get it means breaking through that fence and nosing around inside. For me that's just not on. And now that we've got our breath back I don't think we should stand around chewing the rag out here, because some rather nasty people may come looking for us with the worst of intentions.'

'Come on then.'

The rain was pelting down now and the flashes of lightning were all around, the cracks of thunder almost merging into one another to create a single prolonged concerto from nature's orchestra. It was, Brady thought, one hell of a night to be out and about, even without the probability of having people with guns hunting for them.

They left the belt of scrub and headed towards the road on a course that would take them away from the lighted compound, and it was heavy going. Under the downpour the ground was rapidly becoming waterlogged and soggy, so that their feet made a squelching sound as they ran. It was as if at each step something took a grip on those feet and they had to be dragged free, making a glutinous, sucking sound in the process.

When at last they came to the road Brady was gasping for breath and there was a pain in his side. He had not done much running lately and he was ill prepared for the exercise in such unhelpful conditions. He noticed that Linda seemed to be doing rather better than he was; but she was lighter on her feet and maybe hers did not sink in so deeply. Whatever the reason, she had reached the road well ahead of him and had stopped to allow him to catch up. Which was considerate of her, he thought.

'Now,' she said, 'we've got to find the car.'

It was more easily said than done. The belt of scrub in which they had hidden it was featureless in the darkness, and without a marker to guide them they could only make a guess at the whereabouts of its place of concealment.

'We should have left it in the open,' Brady said. 'And to hell with the risk.'

But it was a trifle late to think of that now, and Linda told him so. 'I didn't hear you mention it at the time.'

It was a flash of lightning that helped them in the end. In this brief illumination Brady caught a glimpse of what he felt sure was the tail of the Beetle. They ran towards the spot and found that it was indeed there.

'Now let's be on our way,' he said.

They wasted no more time in getting into the car, with Linda in the driving seat. Then the engine failed to start and Brady had visions of being stranded there while a search party streamed out from the compound to pick them up and maybe deal with them as ruthlessly as they had dealt with the helicopter and the unfortunate Harold Garfield.

But it came to life at last, and Linda backed the car out on to the road and pointed it in the right direction. Then they were on their way and the road, rapidly turning to a muddy track under the rain with all the potholes brimming with water, lay ahead like a glistening ribbon in the headlights.

'I'm certainly glad to be away from there,' Brady said. 'And if I never see the place again it'll be soon enough for me. It got very nasty for a time.'

'You don't have to tell me,' Linda said. 'I was there too, you know.' She spoke snappishly, and he wondered whether her nerves had been as frayed as his. Maybe. She was human, after all.

But they had got away unscathed, apart from the scratches, and that was the main thing. He had a vision of the inn waiting for them in Acapurno; and that unassuming hostelry had never appeared so attractive as it did in his mind's eye.

This feeling of euphoria lasted for perhaps ten minutes. That was the length of time it took for him to realize that they were being followed.

'Damn!' Linda said. 'They're on our tail.'

It was a straight piece of road and the headlights of the vehicle behind were picking out the Beetle and flashing in the rear-view mirror. She put her foot down on the accelerator pedal and got a few more knots out of the car, but sheer speed had never been one of the attributes of this particular Volkswagen model, and an old and much used one such as they were travelling in at the moment was never going to stay ahead of the pursuit for long.

'They're catching up,' Brady said.

'Now tell me something I don't know.'

It came up fast, really motoring. It was a big pick-up truck; maybe the one they had seen going out to the burning helicopter; and it had a handy turn of speed. A few moments later it had caught them, but the driver made no attempt to pass. They felt the shock as it hit the rear of the Beetle.

Brady looked back through the rear window, and the front of the pick-up was entirely blocking the view, its lights dazzling. It fell back a little and then accelerated hard, coming up fast for a second go at the Beetle's tail.

'Damn it!' Linda said, fighting to stay in control of the car. 'What are they trying to do?'

Brady felt sure she needed no answer to that. It was obvious that whoever was driving the pick-up had it in mind to run them off the road. This became even more evident when, instead of doing any more of the tail-bumping, he tried a new manoeuvre, bringing the truck up beside the car and hitting it sideways. Linda had a real struggle this time to keep the Beetle on the road, and Brady felt pretty sure that sooner or later if the other driver kept using these tactics he was bound in the end to achieve his object.

He could see into the cab of the pick-up when it came alongside, and he caught a glimpse of the two men sitting in it. They were rather shadowy figures because there was no light on in the cab, but this fact seemed to make them even more menacing than they might have been if they had been seen more clearly.

The Beetle came to a bend in the road where it skirted one of the marshy places, and here the front bumper of the pick-up caught it midway along the side. It was the killer punch; there was nothing that Linda could do to prevent the car from going off the road and into the bog. The wheels sank in up to the axles and all forward motion ceased, the rear wheels spinning and throwing up mud but getting no grip in the marshy ground.

Linda switched off the ignition and the sound of the engine died away into silence.

'This is it, Steve,' she said. 'This is the pay-off.'

She sounded calm; no cursing, no bewailing a cruel fate, just an unemotional acceptance of the situation as it was.

The truck had come to a halt a few yards ahead. Now it went into reverse and backed to a point just behind the spot where the Beetle had left the road and become stuck, its headlights illuminating the scene. A man got out of the cab and walked forward into the light, and Brady was surprised to see that he had a Nordic look about him. He was thick-set and his face was bony, his nose more inclined to the snub than the aquiline, blond hair cropped short.

He walked with a kind of swagger, and what made him a most unwelcome sight to the two persons in the Beetle was the fact that he was carrying a gun; a submachine-gun, to be precise.

Brady and Linda were still sitting in the car when he came up to it. He stopped and looked in at them, and then he made a beckoning gesture with his left forefinger which was an unmistakable invitation, or indeed an order, to them to leave the vehicle. Neither of them made any immediate move to do as he wished, and suddenly he stepped back and fired a brief burst with the gun into the side of the car, which, if they had been sitting in the back, would have done them no good at all. It might even have been the last thing they ever had done to them.

The blond man took two more paces back and again made a beckoning gesture, this time, as if to add emphasis to the invitation, with the gun.

'We'd better do what he wants,' Brady said. 'He may have a short temper.'

Linda did not argue with this. Next time the man with the gun might turn his attention to the front of the car, and that would be very far from pleasant for those still sitting in it.

Brady was on the side away from the gunman, and he opened the door and stepped out. His feet immediately sank in and the mud came up to his ankles. He did not see Linda get out, but when he had made his way through the mire to the back of the car he could see that she had also got out and was standing on the road.

Things began to happen very quickly then. She had come to

a halt a couple of yards from the man, and he said something to her which Brady failed to catch; it might have been an order for her to come closer, and he made another gesture with the submachine-gun which he was holding in his right hand only. She took one step, as if in obedience to his order, and suddenly the Smith & Wesson was in her hand. Until that moment the hand and the gun had been concealed under the cuff of her jacket. She must have taken it out of the shoulder bag and cocked it while still in the car, for it fired at once when she squeezed the trigger, which no doubt was very pleasing to her.

She fired twice in quick succession, and the blond man gave a curiously high-pitched scream and dropped the submachine-gun as if it had suddenly become red-hot. His right arm was hanging limply and blood was already beginning to pump out of it just above the bicep muscle where at least one of the bullets must have gone in. Nice shooting, Linda!

'Get the gun, Steve,' she said. 'Quick!'

Brady came round the tail of the car fast, in spite of the mud. He picked up the submachine-gun just as the man who had driven the truck got out from behind the wheel and appeared in the doorway of the cab, a pistol in his hand. He was a black-haired, dark-skinned man and might well have been one of the Arabs, but that was immaterial at the moment. He never got round to using his gun, because Brady fired a burst over his head and he went back in like a rabbit into its burrow.

Linda spoke to the blond man, and there was a snap in her voice and maybe a trace of steel too.

'Get back in there,' she said; and she made a gesture with her pistol to indicate that she meant the cab of the pick-up. 'And then get to hell out of here before you get another shot in the arm or somewhere worse.'

The swagger had all gone out of him now, and he looked sick. He was muttering what might have been curses, but he was not too sick to climb into the cab even with one arm hanging uselessly and dripping with blood. Brady gave him a shove to help him up and slammed the door on him. He kept the submachine-gun in his hands for the present.

The Arab had already restarted the engine, and he was not slow to turn the truck and head back the way it had come. Brady and Linda stood in the road and watched it go. The storm had passed and it had stopped raining even before the Beetle had been forced into the marsh. It was still there, stuck in the mud with the lights on, and there was no hope of getting it out. Now and then a flicker of lightning in the distance would be followed by a faint rumble of thunder like an old man mumbling in his beard of youthful glories long since faded away and gone for ever. But if the weather was no longer a bother to them, there was much else to worry about.

'Steve,' Linda said, 'we're in a fix.'

There could be no doubt about that. They were miles from Acapurno, with no transport and still too close for comfort to the mysterious establishment in the other direction. There was no certainty that when the blond man and the Arab arrived back there and told their story another and bigger force would not be sent out to finish the job which those two had failed to complete. Indeed, it was only too probable that this would happen.

'Too true,' Brady said. 'I'd say this is far from being the healthiest spot to be in right now. I suggest we start walking, or maybe even running, though personally I don't feel in the best of shape for a spell of athletics.'

'I'll switch those car lights off first,' Linda said. 'maybe we can get some help from the garage in Acapurno to haul it out of the filth tomorrow.'

'We're going to have sore feet by then. My God! Do you realize how far we are from civilization?'

'Of course I do. But there's no use moaning about it. And once we reach the main road we may be able to thumb a lift.'

'Judging by the amount of traffic on that road, I'd say it's a pretty slim chance. Especially at night.'

'Well, do you have any better suggestion?'

He had not. He watched her as she squelched to the Beetle, switched off the lights and pocketed the keys. Not that anyone was likely to steal the car, he thought. It was probably as safe there as it would have been in a locked garage.

'Right then,' Linda said. 'Let's start walking.'

But they had not yet taken more than a couple of steps when they saw the headlights of a vehicle coming from the direction of the other road.

'Oh my God!' Brady said. 'Here's more trouble.'

Chapter Eighteen
CARDS ON THE TABLE

It had to be trouble. Because any vehicle travelling on that road in that direction had to be going to the place they had so recently left: the set-up behind the chain-link fence. And anyone going there and seeing two people stranded on the road would be almost bound to stop and ask awkward questions.

'What do we do now?' Brady said. 'Run for cover?'

'What cover?' Linda spoke scathingly. There was the marsh on one side and open country on.the other. 'Talk sense.'

He could see that she had a point. She always did have a point.

'So we stay put?'

'We stay put.'

They were standing at the side of the road. There would have been plenty of room for the approaching vehicle to go past if the driver had so wished; but this was never likely. A car mired in the bog and two people standing nearby would have been too interesting a situation simply to be ignored and driven by with, as it were, averted gaze. Inevitably, the vehicle came to a halt some twenty yards away from them.

They were in the full glare of the headlights and it was difficult to see just what kind of vehicle it was, but somehow it did not look like a car. The dark bulk of it loomed in the shadow behind the lights and it could have been a lorry or a van.

Somebody got out of the cab, and of this person too there was difficulty in making out more than a hazy outline. But then the person moved towards them into the glare of the headlights and said:

'Hey! What is it with you folks? Why the artillery? I'm on your side.'

It was Petersen and the vehicle had to be his motor caravan, his home on wheels. Brady relaxed and lowered the submachine-gun which he had been pointing in the direction of the newcomer. Linda still had the pistol in her hand also. Petersen, seeing these weapons aimed at him, had had some reason for alarm.

He walked towards them and glanced at the stranded Beetle.

'Looks like you had some trouble. Was it just a case of rank bad driving or something else?'

'It was something else,' Linda said.

'You going to tell me?'

'Why not? We were chased by two unpleasant characters in a pick-up truck. They ran us off the road into the bog.'

'Uh-huh!' Petersen took a closer look at the Beetle. 'There's some holes in the bodywork. What made them?'

'Would you believe termites?'

'I'd have difficulty.'

'It was this gun,' Brady said.

'You took potshots at your own buggy?'

'No. The gun was in other hands then.'

'And you took it from those hands? Boy, that must've taken some doing.'

'It didn't. He dropped the gun. All I had to do was walk over and pick it up.'

'Why'd he drop it?'

'He had a pain in his arm.'

'Musta been some pain to make him do that.'

'It was. Linda put a bullet in it. Maybe two. He was bleeding like a stuck pig when he and his pal decided to head for home.'

'My, oh my!' Petersen said. 'I'd like to hear more of this. Sure sounds mighty interesting.'

'Not now,' Linda said. 'There could be others coming along to finish the job.'

'I guess you're right. I could give you both a lift, but I reckon you'd rather have your own car.'

'We would. But as you see, it's stuck.'

'No problem. I got a tow-rope. I can haul it out.'

He walked back to the van, got in and drove it past the spot where the Beetle was mired. The tow-rope he produced was nylon, very strong. He stepped into the mud and attached one end to the rear of the car and the other to the towbar of the van. He got back in the cab and drove forward slowly in low gear. The Beetle resisted for a moment and then came out of the mud with a sound rather like a kid sucking up the last drops of a soft drink through a straw. Then it was back on the road. Petersen stopped the van, got out and retrieved the tow-rope.

'I think we should have a talk,' he said. 'A real heart-to-heart. What d'you say?'

'All right,' Linda said. 'But not here.'

'No, not here. You go ahead and when we get to town we'll have that talk in my van. OK?'

'OK,' Linda said.

She got into the Beetle and it started with no trouble at all this time. Apart from the mud on the wheels and the bullet-holes and the dents in the bodywork, it was, if not as good as new, at least almost as good as it had been before it was pushed off the road. Before he got in on the passenger side Brady threw the submachine-gun as far as he could into the marsh.

'Now why did you do that?'

'Why wouldn't I do it?'

'You might want it again.'

'Wrong. I'll never want it again. It wasn't mine and I didn't want it in the first place.'

'Steve Brady,' she said, 'you're an idiot.'

'I know. And that's why you love me so much, isn't it?'

She made no reply to that. She let the clutch in and got the Beetle moving. Glancing over his shoulder, Brady could see Petersen's mobile home following close behind. There was no sign of any pursuit and he was happy that this was so. He hoped he was seeing the last of that stretch of road and what lay at the end of it; but he had doubts about this. Moreover, he had an uneasy feeling that a certain Rex Petersen might be about to put a fresh slant on things. In what way he could not guess, but the feeling was there none the less.

They came to the junction and turned in the direction of Acapurno, and Petersen followed.

'I wonder,' Brady said, 'what he wants to talk about.'

'I can't imagine,' Linda said. And he did not believe her; he credited her with a lot more imagination than that.

'What on earth was he doing on that piece of road at this time of night?'

'How would I know?'

'One thing's for sure: he wasn't taking photographs for the *National Geographic*.'

'Oh,' she said, 'that's obvious. But then I never did believe that story. Not for a minute.'

'You didn't?'

'Of course not. Did you?'

'As a matter of fact, I did.'

'Oh, Steve,' she said, 'you're so gullible; you really are.'

He resented that. Was it being gullible when somebody told you something not immediately to suspect they were lying? But he saw no point in arguing the matter. He wondered whether Petersen was gullible too. He rather suspected that the man was not.

The talking took place in Petersen's caravan which he had parked in its usual place in the plaza in Acapurno. Compared with the one in which Harold Garfield had been living before his untimely death, this was quite simply luxurious. In the limited space available it seemed to have everything one might need while travelling around. And this included what looked like some very high-tech radio equipment.

The first thing Petersen did when he had welcomed them into this wandering home of his was to produce a bottle of genuine Scotch whisky and pour tots for all.

'You folks look like you could use something to warm the cockles, and that's the truth.'

They were certainly in a bedraggled state. They had been drenched by rain and their feet were coated with mud from the bog. So the spirit was more than welcome, as well as being unexpected.

'Keep a bottle of it for special occasions,' Petersen explained. 'Don't want you to get the idea that I'm a secret boozer.'

'And this is a special occasion?' Linda said.

'Oh, sure. This is where we all get to put our cards on the table and come clean about ourselves. OK?'

'And you think we've got something to come clean about?'

'Heck, yes. Look at it this way. What harmless pair of tourists would go driving out into the night and get themselves barged off the road into a bog before coming to grips with a pair of tough characters with guns and sending these toughies packing? Tell me that, if you please.'

'Well, if it comes to that,' Linda said, 'how did an innocent American photographer, working for the *National Geographic* as ever was, suddenly appear on the scene at a most opportune moment?'

Petersen laughed. '*Touché*, as they say in fencing, so I've heard. Well, I'll tell you. This innocent photographer went looking for you at the inn where you're staying and was told by the landlord that you'd gone off in your car. He didn't know where, so he couldn't tell me. And then this aforementioned innocent shutterbug made a wild guess at where you might have gone and decided to follow.'

'Why?'

'Because it's my belief we're in the same game and could maybe co-operate some. That's why.'

'And what game would that be?' Linda asked softly; her eyes searching Petersen's face.

'Why, the undercover game, of course; the secret agent caper. What else?'

'Are you telling me you're in the CIA?'

'Would it surprise you?'

Linda smiled. 'Oddly enough, no.'

'And you, of course, are British Intelligence. MI5 or is it MI6? You're not going to deny it, are you?'

It was on the tip of Brady's tongue to utter a firm denial, but he had hardly begun to open his mouth when Linda spoke for the two of them.

'No,' she said, 'we're not going to deny it.'

So Brady shut his mouth again and kept it shut; though he could see where this was leading; he could see it only too clearly. And he was not happy about it. There were so many things that kept cropping up which he did not like. Sometimes he wondered whether it would not have been better for his peace of mind if he had never met Miss Manning again; but even now, even with all the jangling of the nerves that association with her seemed inevitably to bring with it, he could not bring himself to regret that meeting. She had him in this spell and he could neither break free from it nor truly wish to do so.

And then Petersen said: 'So now that it's all out in the open, why don't we join forces and play this thing out together? I could sure use a bit of help.'

And Linda said: 'Sure. Why not?'

And Brady said nothing.

Chapter Nineteen

BEST LAID SCHEME

'The object of mutual interest,' Petersen said, 'is of course that set-up behind the ring fence. My guess is you'd been there, doing a bit of nocturnal investigation, when they got on to you. Am I right?'

'You're right,' Linda said.

'You know what's going on in there?'

'No. Do you?'

'I could make a guess.'

'So you don't think it's just a harmless factory doing what factories do?' Brady said.

'Is it likely? If you're going to build a factory in Paraguay, which seems unlikely in the first place, you don't go out into the wilds miles from anywhere to do it. No facilities, nothing. Have to generate your own electricity, bringing the fuel in by truck on pretty dodgy roads; have to dig wells for water; all that sort of thing. Very inconvenient and costly. And why the armed guards? And if it's a factory why do no products ever come out?'

'How do you know nothing comes out?'

'I've asked around. People would know.'

'We heard that too,' Linda said. 'Loaded lorries go in, empty lorries come out. Doesn't make sense.'

'So you see. And then there are the Arabs.'

'You know about them?'

'Sure. And they seem to be the bosses. What would you deduce from that?'

'That the place is under Arab ownership, maybe?'

'No maybe about it in my opinion. Now which country in the Middle East would be likely to build a research station, say, in Paraguay, where the operators wouldn't be forever harassed by British and American warplanes snooping on them and dropping bombs if they sensed anything the least bit suspicious? Like the possible development of chemical and biological weapons, for example? Does anything spring to mind? A name maybe?'

'You're talking about Saddam Hussein, of course.'

'None other. Out here would be so much safer than Iraq. So what better place than this to build the station and get to work? The scientists and technicians and suchlike would be living on the base and carrying out their research and development in perfect safety.'

'Now hold on a minute,' Brady said. 'This is all supposition, isn't it? Have you any proof?'

'Nothing solid. But plenty of circumstantial evidence. I'm pretty damn sure in my own mind that I'm right.'

'But how would they have been able to come here and build the place without the Paraguayan authorities, the government and so on, knowing anything about it? Are you suggesting that they connived at the undertaking?'

'Not knowingly, maybe. It would obviously be presented as a

perfectly harmless establishment, possibly doing research for the good of mankind, that sort of thing. Though I guess there may be some people in high places who've had their palms greased in order to ease things through and no questions asked.'

Linda gave a snap of the fingers. 'The man in grey.'

Petersen glanced questioningly at her. 'Man in grey?'

'There was this man in a grey suit. He came down here, probably from Asunción, and ordered our release after we'd spent a night in the cells on suspicion of having murdered Harold Garfield. He certainly had authority; the police here were in awe of him; he had them jumping out of their skins. And now the whole affair seems to have been hushed up. That has to be significant, wouldn't you say?'

'And you think it was the Arab lot who killed Garfield?'

'I don't see there's any doubt about that.'

'This Harold Garfield,' Petersen said. 'What was your interest in him?'

'He was the one who first passed on to us information about that place which is of such interest to you as well as to us. He'd been nosing around for some time.'

'Ah, I see. He was your man in the field.'

'You could call him that.'

Brady glanced at her and gave a lift of the eyebrows. Now she was giving Petersen the impression that Garfield had been another British Intelligence agent. And it was just not true. There might have been some dead wood in that lot from time to time, but a slob like Harold Garfield would never have stood a chance of getting taken on.

But again he said nothing.

'So Garfield was getting a shade too close for comfort and

they rubbed him out. Well, well! Just goes to show that those guys will stop at nothing to hide their tracks.'

'There's something else which proves that,' Linda said. 'Something that happened before he was killed.'

'What was that?'

'When we were at the place the other day, taking a look at it from cover, a helicopter came over, flying low.'

Petersen's head jerked up. 'That so?'

'Yes. It was quite a small machine and it made a couple of runs over the compound as if whoever was in it might have been taking aerial photos. It was on its fourth pass over the place that the people on the ground shot it down.'

'They shot it down!' Petersen was almost shouting. 'What with?'

'Rifles, machine-guns, the lot. They set it on fire and it went down some way beyond the perimeter fence. Then they went out with a mechanical digger and buried what was left. We had a look at the place tonight with a torch, and we could see where they'd done it.'

Petersen had got up from his seat and it was easy to see that the news had really shocked him. His fists were clenched so hard the knuckles showed white, as if he would have liked to hit out at someone and was frustrated by the lack of a target.

'The bastards! The goddam stinking bastards!'

'That chopper,' Linda said. 'You know something about it?'

'You betcha life I do. I was working with the guys who were in it. I've been trying to get in touch with them.' He indicated the radio equipment with a flick of the hand. 'I wondered why I couldn't get an answer. Now I know. No chance anyone survived?'

Linda shook her head. 'I doubt it.'

'Well,' Petersen said, 'this puts the seal on it. Now I know what I have to do. No more pussyfooting around. Time's past for that. They've asked for it and now they're going to get it. In the neck.'

'What are you proposing to do?' Brady asked.

Petersen glared at him, as though he were a stand-in for the enemy that was out of his reach – for the moment. 'What am I proposing to do! I'll tell you. I'm going to blow that place to hell, that's what. I'm going to make damn sure there's no more research and development of any kind done out there. And if a lot of the swine get blown up too, so much the better.'

He stopped talking, sat down again and drank some more of the whisky, still burning with anger but getting it under control.

Brady said: 'And how do you intend to set about doing that? Have you got the necessary material?'

'Oh, sure. Take a look at this.'

Petersen got up and slid back a panel under the settee on which he had been sitting. The door of a safe was revealed. He worked the combination lock and opened it, revealing some white plastic bags as well as various other articles.

'Guess what's in the bags.'

'I'm no good at guessing,' Brady said.

'And you're going to tell us anyway,' Linda said. 'So come on. What is it?'

'OK. No games then. It's Semtex.'

'Now I wonder,' Linda said, 'why that doesn't really surprise me. Where'd you get the stuff?'

Petersen laid a finger along the side of his nose. 'Ask no questions and you'll be told no lies. You can get anything, even in a place like Asunción, if you know the right people to contact and you have the dollars.'

'And you have the dollars, of course.'

'The people I work for have. I can draw what I need.'

'Lucky you.'

'There's detonators and timers in there too.'

'All the necessary gear for a real big bang.'

'Or more than one,' Petersen said. He closed and relocked the safe, slid the panel across to hide it and sat down again. 'That plastic explosive is the goods. A little goes a long way.'

'You've used it before?'

'On occasion.'

Brady was feeling more and more uneasy. He could see what he and Linda were being drawn into, and it was going to be hellishly risky. But he could tell that Linda was all for it. It was becoming more and more like the old times for her. No doubt the prospect of it set the blood coursing through her veins, while all he could think of was the possibility of a lot of that bright red liquid spilling out of them.

'There's the little matter of getting through the fence,' she said. 'I suppose you've thought of that?'

'Yes, I've thought of it. I've a pair of bolt cutters that'll go through that chain-link like a hot knife through butter.'

'There's a place where a thicket of bushes and small trees grows quite close to the fence. We found it when we were there. It could be the best place to go in. It gives a bit of cover.'

'Sounds reasonable.'

'There are guard dogs,' Brady said. 'Dobermans. Nasty brutes.'

'How many?'

'Two is all we saw.'

'No problem,' Petersen said. He seemed very confident.

'Well, if you say so.'

'When do you plan to go in?' Linda asked.

Petersen thought about it. Then: 'I guess tonight's ruled out. How about tomorrow? Get there about midnight. Should be most of them in bed by then. That OK with you?'

'I don't see why not,' Linda said.

'You're crazy,' Brady said. 'Just plain crackers, the pair of you. You know that, don't you?'

Petersen grinned at him, and there was a kind of fierceness in the grin. 'Does it bother you, pal?'

'You bet your sweet American life it bothers me. Getting myself involved with two nutcases, why wouldn't it?'

'Take no notice, Rex,' Linda said. 'He's always like this. It's his nature. But he comes good when the going gets rough.'

Petersen said: 'You still got that gun you took off the other guy, Steve?'

'No,' Brady said. 'I threw it away.'

'The hell you did! Why?'

'I don't like guns.'

Petersen looked amazed, even horrified. 'You're in this kinda game and you don't like guns?'

Brady wanted to tell him that he was not in that kind of game and never had been by choice; only by force of circumstance and more than a little arm twisting. But he doubted whether Linda would have liked it. He could have told Petersen also that he had once killed a CIA man – quite by accident of course – not knowing until later that he was one of that lot. And then he and a man named Wilkinson – and where was he now? – had tipped the body out of a boat into a lake in what was then Soviet Russia, all in the middle of the night. Ah, those happy, happy days of long ago! Happy? Like hell they were! Except in parts, of course. For there had been sweet, blissful interludes, moments of sheer delight squeezed in between those others that scared the living daylights out of him.

But why tell Petersen any of this? Petersen who probably regarded his dislike of guns as some horrible disease like leprosy or bubonic plague.

'That one who was using the gun,' Linda said, 'the one I shot in the arm; he looked like a German.'

'Is that a fact?' Petersen said. 'Well, I guess he could have been. A mercenary, maybe. On the other hand, he could have been Paraguayan. A lot of Germans emigrated to this country years ago and I guess there are descendants who've inherited the looks.'

'Well, it's not important. One more question. Have you figured out where you're going to plant the explosive when we get inside the fence?'

'Sure. Let me show you. It would have been better if I had those photographs the guys in the chopper were taking, but I guess this is not far out.'

He took a folded sheet of paper from a pocket and spread it out on the small table with which the caravan was provided. Linda and Brady stood up and looked at it. It was a rough plan of the buildings inside the ring fence, some of which had been marked with crosses.

'Those are the ones I think are important. Now where is this place in the fence you reckon we should go through?'

Linda pointed it out. 'About there.'

Petersen drew a line with a pencil from the spot she had indicated to the nearest of the main buildings he had marked, and from that to the others.

'This is the way we'll go. OK?'

'Looks fine to me,' Linda said.

'The best-laid schemes of mice and men,' Brady murmured.

Linda told him to shut up before he ever got to the 'Gang aft a-gley' part of the quotation. But it was in his mind.

Chapter Twenty

NIGHT WORK

It was late when they returned to the inn, and the only customers left, if they could have been called that, were three men who were playing cards with the landlord at the dining-table. The arrival of the two guests attracted some attention from the card-players. It was their bedraggled appearance that caused it, for though they had dried out to some extent in Petersen's caravan and had managed to get rid of a good deal of the mud that had been clinging to them, they still looked rather the worse for wear.

The *señora*, coming in at that moment from the kitchen, raised her hands in horror.

'What has happened? Have you had an accident?'

Linda explained that they had lost their way in the darkness and had been caught in a thunderstorm.

'You were not in your car?'

'Not just then. We had gone for a walk.'

It sounded an unlikely story. That anyone should go for a drive at a late hour, and then should leave their car and go walking was surely the craziest thing. But perhaps it would be accepted. They were foreigners after all and might be expected to act in the oddest of ways. They were, of course, also the couple who had been falsely arrested by those animals, the police, and forced to spend a night in captivity, and as such were entitled to a degree of respect.

Their coming in broke up the card party; the three men departed, leaving them with the innkeeper and his wife. Señora Cortés fussed over them like a hen with chicks. She was sure they must be famished, and she insisted on heating up some soup for them, while Cortés himself opened a bottle of wine. It was all so very different from the rather cool reception they had had on their first arrival at the inn. It was quite amazing what a falling out with the local constabulary could do for one's standing in certain places.

They were in bed when Brady asked a question that had been in his mind for some time.

'Why did you tell Petersen we were in British Intelligence?'

'I didn't,' she said.

'You said you were not going to deny it.'

'That doesn't mean I was saying we were.'

'It was tantamount to saying so.'

'Oh,' she said, 'to hell with tantamount.'

'To hell with it if you like. But see where it's got us. Now we're committed to going with him on this hare-brained project of blowing up those buildings.'

'You think it's hare-brained?'

'Yes, I do. Don't you?'

'Frankly, no. I think it's something that needs doing. That place is a threat to all of us and needs to be knocked out.'

'You don't know that. It's only a theory.'

'A theory that's got a lot of evidence to support it. You must admit that.'

She was right there, he thought; but he still did not see why they had to take it upon themselves to do what was necessary. Why could not Rex Petersen just send in a report to his people in Washington and leave it to them to deal with the problem? Why did he have to do the job himself? Because he was crazy, that was why. And they were crazy to go in with him; they surely were. Yet they were going to do it. Tomorrow they were going to put their lives on the line and they could all end up like Harold Garfield and the men in the helicopter. It was a pleasant prospect.

So why didn't he do the sensible thing and worm out of it? Why didn't he say enough was enough and he was not going a step further? Because of Linda, of course. She was the reason. Always had been and maybe always would be as long as he stayed with her.

'Now look,' he said. 'Why don't we talk this thing over? Why don't we go to Petersen tomorrow and tell him we've had second thoughts? Hell, why don't we tell him we're not in British Intelligence? Tell him that was all over long ago. What do you say?'

She said nothing. She was asleep.

They went in Petersen's caravan. There was room for all of them in the front. They had told Cortés they were going to spend the evening with some people they had met in town and it might be very late when they came back. Cortés had said that would be all right. There was a bell, and if they rang it he or somebody else would come down and let them in even if they had already gone to bed.

So now here they were on their way and he had been told what his job was. Since he had no gun, he was going to be a porter and carry the bag with the four bombs in it that Petersen had prepared. Nice work, Brady!

'I suppose,' he said, 'there's no chance of these bombs going off while I'm carrying them?'

'Look on the bright side,' Petersen said. 'If they do, you won't know anything about it.'

Which was very reassuring.

'I just hope it doesn't rain,' he said.

'That's right,' Linda said. 'Always the happy little optimist, Steve Brady. It's not going to rain.'

'How do you know? Have you heard a weather forecast?'

'I feel it in my bones.'

'All I feel in my bones is a touch of the rheumatics. Could be the result of that soaking we had last night.'

'You're getting old, Steve,' she said.

'Aren't we all?'

They left the caravan partially screened by scrub where they had left Garfield's Shogun and the Beetle. It was close on midnight and the sky was almost cloudless, with just a wafer of moon showing amid a host of stars. Brady had the canvas bag with the bombs in it slung on his shoulder with a strap. It was not as heavy as he would have expected, but of course these modern plastic explosives were very concentrated and you needed less of them to produce as much effect as a greater weight of the older stuff. Barrels of gunpowder had been all very well for Guy Fawkes, but there had been a lot of progress in that field since the abortive plot to blow up the Houses of Parliament and good King James. He just hoped Petersen knew what he was doing with the Semtex. He would have hated to be hoist with his own petard; though the fact was that he had never been quite sure what a petard was. Something rather nasty, no doubt.

Petersen was carrying the bolt-cutters in another bag, and he almost certainly had a gun. Linda had her shoulder bag, presumably with the little Smith & Wesson which she had already used to such good effect. Now it had come to the crunch, he half regretted that he had thrown the submachine-gun away. It was true that he was no lover of guns, but there were times when they came in handy, and this might be one of them. Still, it was too late to think about that now.

They kept well away from the fence as they approached the belt of scrub. The compound was on their left and there were a few lights showing, but not in the buildings.

'With luck,' Petersen said, 'we'll catch them all asleep.'

Brady did not believe it, and he doubted whether Petersen did either; it would have been too much to hope for.

The ground under foot was still soft and squelchy after the previous night's rain, but not as bad as it had been then. They came level with the thicket and turned and walked towards it where it appeared as a black, ill-defined shape in the faint light.

Then they were moving through it, and the thorns were catching them and they were stumbling on the roots and brambles, but still making progress towards the fence. They came to it and could see no one moving around on the inside.

'Looks like we could be lucky,' Petersen said.

He set to work at once with the bolt-cutters, and he had not been at it for more than a minute when the dogs came running. They were at the fence pretty quickly, and they were snarling like mad and barking a little, and one of them managed to get its muzzle through the bottom of the netting where Petersen had cut some of the wire. He had dropped the cutters as soon as he saw the dogs and had taken something else out of the bag. It looked to Brady like a big pistol, but when he fired it there was just a slight coughing sound and he knew that it was the kind that used compressed air as a propellant.

The dog that had pushed its muzzle through the fence gave a yelp and drew back. It moved away to one side, but it seemed unsteady on its legs, as though the strength had gone out of them. A moment later it had collapsed.

Petersen had already loaded the air-pistol with another dart and again the pistol gave a cough and the second dog yelped and staggered away before collapsing on the ground. Petersen put the gun away and resumed work with the cutters.

Brady could see now why the American had been so confident that the dogs would present no problem. He appeared to be equipped for every contingency. An air-pistol with some drugged darts was a useful weapon when there were guard dogs around.

Soon Petersen had cut a hole in the fence large enough for them to crawl through, and the brief barking of the dogs appeared not to have raised any alarm. He put the cutters back in the bag with the air-pistol and left it there.

'OK. Let's go.'

He went through first, followed by Linda, with Brady bringing up the rear and carrying the explosives. The scattered lights in the compound gave only a partial illumination to the area, but there was one not far from the stretch of tarmac which they had to cross to reach the nearest of the buildings Petersen had pin-pointed as being those where the critical work was in all probability carried out. There were four of these; they were separate from one another but were arranged in a square so that they enclosed a quadrangle.

Brady's heart was thumping as they ran across the open ground, expecting at any moment to hear a challenge or, worse still, the sound of a shot. But nothing of this kind happened; all seemed quiet in the compound, and they reached the first building and paused in a huddle against its outer wall. Still all was silent, as if everyone was soundly sleeping. It seemed unbelievable that in such a place there would be no night-watchmen; that all would be left to the guard dogs. But of course night-watchmen had been known to sleep on duty.

'Let's go round to the other side,' Petersen said.

Again he led the way and they came round into the quadrangle, keeping close to the wall and on the alert for anyone who might be moving around at that time of night. And there was no one. It really seemed too good to be true.

The light was dimmer in that enclosed area, but they could see that the buildings were all built to the same pattern, with a porch enclosing the main doorway at about the middle of the inner wall. This was greatly to Petersen's satisfaction, since the porch was an admirable place in which to plant a bomb.

They all crept into the first porch, and Brady opened the bag he had been carrying. It was so dark in the porch that Linda had to use her torch, shading it with her hand, to give Petersen enough light to set the timer on the bomb. It took only a minute or so, but it seemed like an age to Brady; and then they were moving on to the next building, the next porch, the next planting of a bomb.

They were on the third porch when they heard the sound of footsteps on the tarmac. Linda switched off the torch and they froze. The footsteps came closer, then stopped. Someone was standing still, perhaps at the centre of the quadrangle. He had possibly heard a sound and was taking a good look round the area. Perhaps he had caught a glimpse of the torchlight before it was switched off, and was suspicious. And then it became evident that he had a torch of his own which he was using to aid him in his search. They could see the light from it as the beam moved round the square. It came closer to the porch where they were huddled; in a moment it must reveal them; it would be impossible to avoid detection.

But then they heard a man's voice. He was shouting to the man in the square, and though it was impossible to catch the exact words, the urgency in them was unmistakable. The torchlight went out and the man must have departed, running. They could hear his feet drumming on the tarmac and then he was gone.

'So what was that all about?' Brady said.

'I don't know,' Petersen said. 'But my guess is, somebody found the dogs.'

'So what do we do now?'

'We plant that other bomb, that's what.'

It was the sensible thing to do, of course. There was no point in running for the gap in the fence if the two men had found the dogs. They would see the gap and know that was where,the intruders had come in and where they would try to get out.'

'Bring the bag,' Petersen said.

He started walking towards the last porch and Brady followed with the Semtex. Two minutes later the fourth bomb had been planted and they were ready to leave.

But which way? That was the question.

'Let's take a look at things,' Petersen said.

They moved to the building they had attended to first, and

Petersen took a peep round the corner of it while Linda and Brady stayed behind him.

'That's odd,' Petersen said. He sounded puzzled. 'That's damned odd.'

'What is?' Brady asked.

'They've vanished. Take a look.'

Brady peered round the corner of the building and he could just make out the dogs lying where they had left them, about fifty yards away. He could not discern the gap in the fence, but it had to be there. And there certainly was no sign of either man.

'So maybe they didn't see the dogs. Maybe it was something else that drew their attention.'

Petersen had to admit that it seemed like it.

'Well, what now? Do we make a dash for it and hope nobody shoots us down before we reach cover?'

'I think we should,' Linda said. 'It's our only chance in my opinion.'

Petersen agreed. 'Let's go then.'

In the fifty yard sprint he won by feet. Brady came in last; he felt obliged to let Linda stay ahead of him. And all the way his ear was cocked for the crack of a rifle that might be followed immediately by the smack of a bullet in the back.

But nothing happened.

Until they reached the fence.

Then two men stepped out of the thicket on the other side. They were carrying submachine-guns and the guns were pointing at the three intruders.

Chapter Twenty-One
PRETTY GOOD JOB

It was difficult to see their faces clearly in the gloom, but they were certainly dark-skinned and their hair was black. They were probably Arabs.

Petersen made a move as if to get at a gun, and the man on the right, the bigger of the two, spoke one word sharply: 'Don't!'

And he said it in English.

Petersen may have been a crazy devil, but he was not crazy enough to disobey an order like that when he was staring down the barrel of a submachine-gun. He checked the movement of his hand and then showed both of them, palms forward.

The smaller of the two Arabs scrambled through the hole in the fence and came up on the inside while his companion kept the would-be escapers covered. With the smaller man on the inside and taking over the task of pointing a gun at the intruders, the other man followed him into the enclosure. He said something to the smaller man, possibly in Arabic, and this one did a quick frisking job. He came up with Petersen's handgun and he also found Linda's Smith & Wesson in her shoulder bag.

On Brady he could, for the best of reasons, find no weapon. It seemed to disappoint him a little.

'Now we will all go where we can have a talk,' the bigger man said. He appeared to be the superior of the two.

The three captives were escorted to a smaller building than those which had bombs planted in their porches, and it was some distance away from the nearest of them. Inside they were taken to a room that appeared to be in use as an office. There were two desks, and the bigger Arab, who had a nose like a hawk, laid his gun on one of them and lowered himself on to a chair behind it. The other Arab, who sported a thin moustache, laid the pistols he had taken from Linda and Petersen on this same desk and then took up a standing position with his back to the door, gun in hand.

There were some other chairs in the room, but the captives were not invited to sit on them. Now that Brady was able to see the man with the moustache in a better light he had a feeling that he looked familiar; and then it occurred to him that this was the man who had been driving the pick-up truck that had forced the Beetle off the road and into the marsh. He was not particularly happy to renew the acquaintance with a person who might have very good reason to bear him a grudge.

Meanwhile, the man himself had been staring at him and Linda, and soon it became apparent that he had made the connection too, for suddenly, without any warning, he stepped forward and struck Linda hard on the cheek with the flat of his hand. Then, with scarcely a pause he did the same to Brady. He seemed inclined to repeat the treatment, but the hawk-nosed man rapped out an order, and it stopped him.

Nevertheless, he looked as if he would have wished to do more, and there was a rapid exchange of words between him and his superior, in which he might have been explaining his behaviour.

Brady had been staggered by the stinging blow and Linda had been all but thrown off her feet. The man had struck viciously, and if his intention had been to inflict pain he had succeeded admirably. Brady's cheek burned with the effect and he had been almost goaded into striking back. He had curbed the impulse, aware that nothing would have been gained by doing so and much might have been lost.

The hawk-nosed man turned to him now and said with a rather twisted smile: 'He says he recognizes you and the woman. It was she who shot a man named Lothar in the arm and you who fired a submachine-gun at him.'

'Not at him,' Brady said. 'If I had done that he would not be talking to you now. I just did it to scare him; and anyway it was he and his pal who started the trouble. They drove us off the road.'

'That may be so; but he is very angry with you. If he had his way he would shoot you both here and now. And the other man.'

'Then I am very glad he is not going to have his way.'

'Do not be so sure of that. There is yet time.'

He picked up a telephone that was on the desk and spoke into it briefly. Brady guessed that he was getting in touch with someone else in the establishment who might perhaps have more authority. He had again been speaking in language that was possibly Arabic.

They waited then; but in this interval of time the man at the desk ordered the other one to search the captives. He did so, but found nothing on any of them to give a clue to their identity. Linda and Brady had left their passports at the inn and

Petersen's was in the safe in his caravan. This search had just been completed when the door opened and another man came in. He was also an Arab, and judging by his appearance he had been roused from sleep and had not waited to dress but had come in haste. He was in pyjamas and a dressing-gown, with slippers on his feet. He was a plump, middle-aged man with a fleshy, pockmarked face, and he did not look pleased.

The man at the desk stood up when this latest arrival entered and surrendered his chair to the newcomer, who sat down and glowered at the captives. Meanwhile the hawk-nosed man stood beside him and gabbled something in his ear which was probably a brief account of how the three intruders had been captured. When he had finished the plump man suddenly snapped out a question in English:

'Who are you?'

It was Petersen who answered: 'Visitors.'

The plump man frowned. 'You are being funny? Believe me, this is not a funny situation. Especially for you. You cut a hole in the perimeter fence and broke in. You killed the guard-dogs.'

'They're not dead. Just put to sleep.'

The plump man made a dismissive gesture with his hand. 'That is not important. What is important is the fact that you broke in. 'Why?'

'We thought we'd like to take a look around the place.'

'In the middle of the night?'

'It seems to be difficult to get in during the day.'

'You are still making a joke of this. And it is no joke. Do you know what I think? I think you are spies. You are here to spy on us. Isn't that so?'

'Why would we do that? Have you something to hide?'

The plump man was becoming more and more angry. He

thumped the desk with his fist. 'Who are you working for? Who sent you?'

'Nobody sent us. It was our own idea.'

The plump man turned to the one standing beside him and said something in Arabic. This man gave a shake of the head and made a gesture with his hands, palms upward.

'So,' the plump man said, turning again to the captives, 'you have nothing on you to reveal your identity. That is significant, wouldn't you say?'

Petersen merely shrugged.

The plump man said: 'You are American. No?'

'Is that what you think?'

To Brady it seemed that Petersen was deliberately trying to goad the interrogator. If so, he was undoubtedly succeeding; the flippant, even contemptuous manner in which he was answering the questions put to him was obviously getting under the plump man's skin. But why was he doing it?

And then it occurred to Brady to wonder just how long it would be before the bombs went off. He had asked Petersen how much time he had allowed when setting the timers, and all the answer he had got was: 'Enough.'

But what did that mean? Enough time for them to get away before the balloon went up? If all had gone according to plan they should have been well clear of the place in no more than ten minutes or so. And of course the shorter the delay, the less likelihood there would have been of a night-watchman discovering the bombs before they exploded.

The snag was that all had not gone according to plan. Things in his experience never did. Generals made detailed plans of battle, and they were never right either. The reason was that no one could look into the future; except maybe the old witches with their crystal balls or their bubbling cauldrons. There was a time when the wise men who advised monarchs cut open chickens to see whether the auguries were good or not; but he doubted whether Petersen would have taken a look at any poultry's entrails even if he had thought of it. He had probably not consulted the stars either, but had just pressed on regardless, in the expectation that long before this the three of them would have been far away from the scene of the crime and on their way back to Acapurno.

Only they were not. Things, as he, Brady, could have foretold if anyone had listened, had not gone according to plan; not by a long chalk. And so here they were being interrogated by this fat character with his tousled hair and his heavy jowl and his silk dressing-gown and Persian slippers while the seconds ticked away and the blobs of Semtex waited for the detonators to give them the go-ahead.

He should never have agreed to take part in such a mad scheme. It had been all against his better judgement, and his better judgement had been spot-on. But of course Linda had been all for it. Why? Some left-over instinct from her days with the Department, that crazy bunch who had sent him on disastrous missions without a clue to what they were all about? Did she have the feeling that in some way she was still working for them, as Petersen obviously believed? Maybe.

So it had come to this: a right bloody mess if ever there was one. And here was Petersen apparently doing his damnedest to goad old pudding-chops into having a heart attack, and to what purpose? He felt like asking the man what the devil he was up to and just when the roof was due to fall in. But perhaps Petersen himself did not know. Maybe he was not so hot at setting bomb-timers as he would have had you think. Maybe he should have taken a course of instruction with the IRA.

The interchange between Petersen and the plump man was still going on, though it had tended to pass over his head, busy as he had been with his thoughts, which were of a rather gloomy nature. But now he became aware that the man was speaking again.

'You are very foolish, you know. We do not take kindly to outsiders meddling in our affairs, as they have this annoying habit of doing. We take stern measures to protect our interests. You must understand that.'

'Oh, I understand it very well,' Petersen said.

'So you see,' the plump man said. And then he paused and struck his forehead with the palm of his right hand, and cried: 'Bombs!' And then he repeated the word on a rising note of shock and dismay: 'Bombs! That is it, that is it!'

The other two looked at him questioningly, not getting the message, and he screamed at them: 'They have planted bombs. That is what they are here for. Search the buildings at once, at once. Hurry!' Then, as though suddenly realizing he had been speaking in English, he switched to Arabic and apparently repeated the warning.

Even then they made no immediate move. They seemed unable to decide just where to start the search, how to organize the procedure. And it would have made no difference anyway. However fast they had moved it would have been too late, all far too late.

Petersen's judgement of what would have been enough time for him and Linda and Brady to get away had been a trifle on the mean side, no doubt about it. The plump man in the silk dressing-gown had just begun to lift his flabby bulk from the chair when the first explosion came. It was one hell of a crack, and though Brady could not tell what effect it had had on the building where it had been planted he knew exactly what it had done to the room they were in. And that was plenty.

The window was shattered, and a piece of flying glass in the shape of a triangle embedded itself in the plump man's neck. He fell back screaming, with blood spurting from the wound. The man with the moustache was slammed back against the door, and it must have given him a smack on the head, for he dropped the gun and just crumpled in a heap on the floor. Linda and Petersen had both been thrown down and the hawk-nosed Arab was lying across the desk, apparently dazed. Brady himself had felt something strike him on the left shoulder; he was not sure what it was, but it brought him to his knees. There was dust and plaster everywhere; a lot of the ceiling had fallen in and cracks had appeared in the walls.

Petersen was the first to recover and come to his senses. He struggled to his feet and helped Linda to get up. Neither appeared to be seriously injured. Brady got up too. There was a singing in his ears and his shoulder ached.

'You OK?' Petersen asked.

'I think so.'

The Arab who had fallen on the desk was recovering. Petersen pulled the guns out of his reach, though he looked far too groggy to be thinking of using any of them. The plump man had fallen off the chair and was on the floor, moaning. Brady thought he looked like a goner with all that blood leaking from his neck.

'Better be going,' Petersen said. He handed one of the submachine-guns to Brady. 'Take this. You may need it.'

Brady took the gun. Maybe it was as well to have one after all – in the circumstances. And it was better in his hands than in the

Arab's. Petersen picked up the gun that was lying on the floor and retrieved the pistols from the desk. He handed the Smith & Wesson to Linda and stowed the other one in a pocket.

'Right then. Let's be on our way.'

The Arab on the floor was still unconscious and blocking the doorway. They had to drag him out of the way, and then they found that the door was jammed. It took the combined efforts of Petersen and Brady to force it open. Then they were in the small lobby and the way was clear, because the outer door had been blown in by the explosion.

As they came out into the open the second bomb went off. Fortunately it was in one of the buildings on the far side of the square and they were shielded from most of the blast by one of those nearer to them. But that too might go up at any moment and it was imperative to get away from there without delay.

In the building where the first bomb had exploded a fire had started somehow and it was finding some highly inflammable material to feed on. There could be no doubt that whatever had been inside it would be completely destroyed. But this was not the time to stand around and reflect on such matters.

'Come on!' Petersen yelled. 'Don't just stand there. Get moving.'

They began to run, with him in the lead. They headed away from the large buildings and ran in the direction of the smaller ones that they had identified as living quarters. Lights were coming on in windows and one or two people had already come outside to see what was going on. The glare of the flames now added its garish light to the scene and a host of sparks was leaping high into the night sky.

Then the third bomb exploded and some pieces of debris fell round about. They were getting nearer to the houses now, and more people had come out to see what was going on. They could hear the babble of voices and some of the people shouted at them, possibly asking questions to which they got no reply. It must have seemed strange to them, seeing three persons running from the shattered buildings and the fire, two of them with guns in their hands. But it was not likely that anyone would attempt to stop them; in the confusion they were safe enough for the present.

When they were about thirty yards from the houses they cut away to the right, still under Petersen's leadership, and headed towards the fence. The fourth and last bomb had just exploded when they reached it. But they were some distance from the point where the gap was, and they had to turn again and run along beside the wire for another hundred yards or so before coming to it.

It was the dogs that marked the place. They were just beginning to stir as the effect of the drug wore off, but they were no threat. Petersen held the wire back for Linda to go through first. Then he followed and Brady brought up the rear. Petersen picked up the bag with the bolt-cutters and the air-pistol in it, which was still lying where he had left it, but Brady had abandoned the bag that had held the bombs a long way back. The two of them were still carrying the submachine-guns, but there was little likelihood of their needing them now. There would be far too much disorder for anyone to think about organizing a pursuit of the bombers.

The thorns tore at them again as they forced their way through the thicket, but very soon they were clear of it and could see that fires were still raging in the compound and making a red glow in the sky.

'Some blaze,' Petersen said. He sounded exultant. 'I didn't

really count on that. It's a bonus. Reckon we did a pretty good job back there.'

But it was not the time to stand around and gloat. There was still that faint possibility that the two Arabs who had captured them might be sufficiently recovered to do something about repeating the exercise. The plump man in the silk dressing-gown could be left out of the reckoning, but the other two might just be a threat.

'Come along,' Brady said. 'We aren't home and dry yet.'

'Right in one,' Petersen agreed. 'Let's beat it.'

They began to run towards the road.

Chapter Twenty-Two

SOME PARTY

Brady was glad to see the dark shape of the motor caravan. His chest was hurting and the left shoulder was giving him some pain also. If there had been much further to run he was not sure he could have made it. But it was amazing what you could do when there was sufficient incentive; and there was plenty of that here; he wanted to get as far away from that damned establishment behind the chain-link fencing as it was possible to be. And he hoped never to see it again.

They all climbed into the cab, and Petersen switched on the ignition and the engine came to life as sweetly as could be. And this was a relief to him too; it would have been one hell of a time for the engine to go on the blink. He just hoped there was plenty of fuel in the tank, but he guessed Petersen had made sure of that.

They were on the road and heading away from the scene of all the mayhem when Brady said: 'I suppose you're feeling pretty happy now.'

'Why wouldn't I?' Petersen said. 'We did it, didn't we? We really gave that place the works. You bet I'm happy.'

'I suppose it doesn't occur to you that you might just possibly have got it wrong?'

'In what way, pal?'

'In the way that we still don't know for certain that what we've destroyed had the least connection with the man in Iraq. There's no proof of it is there? Pal.'

'Well, sure there's no cast-iron, copper-bottomed proof,' Petersen admitted with some apparent reluctance. 'But hell, it's pretty close to a dead cert in my opinion.'

'Yet suppose you're wrong, as you must admit you just could be, then we've blown up something that had nothing whatever to do with Saddam's drive for weapons of mass destruction. Doesn't that bother you at all?'

'Only in the sense that I'd be disappointed at not hitting Saddam's lot. I sure wouldn't be shedding any tears for them we did hit.'

'You wouldn't?'

'Hell, no. Whoever they were, they were up to no good. The goddam bastards shot the helicopter down and killed my buddies. I owed them one for that. And besides, they shot your man Garfield, didn't they? What more justification do you need, for Pete's sake?'

'Garfield wasn't our man,' Brady said. 'Not in the way you mean.'

'Not your man! Then who in hell was he?'

Linda put a word in then. 'What Steve means is that we aren't really working for British Intelligence. I used to be with them years ago in the Cold War days, but not now.'

'And I never was a pukka secret agent,' Brady said. 'I was just an idiot they called in when they wanted a dodgy job done and didn't want to risk one of their regular operators. I was the patsy they could afford to lose.'

'He's bending the truth a bit,' Linda said. 'Really he was very well thought of in the Department.'

'As a sucker,' Brady said. 'In that respect I came through with flying colours.'

'I don't get it,' Petersen said; and he sounded bemused. 'If you're not intelligence agents, why did you say you were?'

'I didn't,' Brady said.

'But Linda did.'

'Not so,' she said. 'All I said was that I wouldn't deny it.'

'Knowing, of course, that I'd take that as an admission that you were. Why?'

'It seemed a good idea at the time.'

'Not to me,' Brady said. 'I wanted to pull out, but I let myself be persuaded to go along with it. I'm still the patsy, you see.'

'So who was this guy Harold Garfield?'

'I don't think we'll go into all that,' Linda said. 'It's a long story and it makes no difference now. The job is finished for all of us. Tomorrow we'll be heading for home and you'll be going wherever it is you're planning to go next. Let's leave it at that, shall we?'

'Sure, let's leave it at that. And thanks for everything.'

'You're welcome.'

They dumped the submachine-guns before they reached the main road. Petersen said he regretted throwing good guns away; it seemed such a waste. But it was best not to have them in the caravan. They threw them as far away from the road as they could and they just vanished into the darkness. Ten minutes later they came to the junction and turned right and headed for Acapurno.

It was still a cool, clear night when they reached the town, and there seemed to be nobody awake. Petersen drove the caravan on to the plaza and parked it in the usual place. He asked the others whether they would like to have some more of the whisky just to round things off, but they declined the offer. Neither of them felt in the mood for celebrating, and Brady for one just felt enormously relieved that the whole wretched business was finished. He also felt thoroughly worn out, and he would have made a guess that Linda did too.

Cortés himself came down to let them in when they rang the doorbell at the inn. He was wearing nothing but a singlet and underpants, and his feet were bare. He seemed still half asleep and appeared not to notice their somewhat unkempt condition.

'You have a good time?' he asked, yawning heavily.

'Sure,' Brady said.

'It was quite a party,' Linda said.

If you liked that kind of party, Brady thought.

When they looked out of the window in the morning they saw that where the motor caravan had been parked there was now an empty space. Petersen had evidently made an early departure.

'That's somebody,' Linda said, 'I doubt whether we shall ever see again.'

'It'll be soon enough for me,' Brady said.

They themselves left as soon as they had had breakfast. There was nothing more to keep them in Acapurno. Cortés and the *señora* appeared quite sorry to see them go. It was perhaps more than the business with the police that had endeared them to the couple. Brady hoped so.

'You will return some day perhaps?' the *señora* said.

'Perhaps,' Brady said. 'Who knows?'

'Indeed, who does? Ah, the uncertainty of life.'

Brady pressed her hand and observed in her eye something that might almost have been a tear, and the slatternly girl wept unrestrainedly to see them go.

No rumour seemed yet to have reached the town of the disaster away to the north. Inevitably the news would leak through eventually, but it might be hushed up. The man in the grey suit might have something to say about it.

Remembering him, Brady felt it might be advisable to get out of the country as quickly as possible, and he was glad that the maltreated Beetle completed the journey to Asunción without mishap.

'What do we do with the car?' Brady asked. 'Do we dump it in a sidestreet or on a bit of waste ground?'

Linda thought this would be unwise.

'Then what?'

'I think we should sell it.'

'Sell it! You propose hawking it round the town looking for a buyer?'

'No,' she said, 'that won't be necessary. I know a man who will buy it.'

The used-car salesman with the sleek black hair and the sideburns and the thin moustache looked at the Beetle and pursed his lips.

'You have treated it badly. In scarcely a week I would not have believed it possible.'

'It is amazing what you can do in a week if you really set your mind to it,' Linda said.

He looked at her as if he could not be certain whether or not she were joking. He moved round the car to view it from all sides, and he kept shaking his head in disapproval.

'It looks as if something hit it in the back. And there are holes in this side panel.' He peered at them more closely. 'They look like bullet-holes.'

'There is a good reason for that,' Linda said.

'Yes?' He looked at her enquiringly. 'What reason would that be?'

'They are bullet-holes.'

'Somebody shot at you?'

'We certainly did not put them there ourselves.'

'You have been attacked? By brigands, perhaps.'

'You might call them that.'

'You are fortunate to be alive.'

'You could say that too.'

'It lowers the value of the car, of course.'

'You don't think somebody might pay a good price to exhibit it to friends and spin a story of fighting off the brigands?'

The man shook his head. 'It is unlikely.'

'So what will you give for it?'

The man pursed his lips again, and then said: 'Ten dollars. American.'

'Ten dollars! A week ago I gave you three hundred and fifty for it.'

'That was before it had been dented in the rear and had bullets shot through the side.'

'But it is not that much damage. Give me a hundred dollars and it's yours.'

He gave a pained kind of smile, as if he could hardly believe what he was hearing. He did not even bother to reject the figure in words. He just waited for the English woman to lower her demand, as he was confident she would.

'Seventy-five.'

The salesman kicked one of the tyres. A little dried mud fell from it.

'Twenty.'

Linda went to the car, opened a door and took the Smith & Wesson self-loader from the glove compartment. The salesman viewed it with alarm, possibly believing that she was going to threaten him with it. He seemed much relieved when she said:

'This is a nearly new gun. It has been fired only twice. It is yours with the car for twenty-five dollars.'

It was the gun that was the clincher. Maybe he was a gun-lover. He counted out the twenty-five dollars and they walked away.

'He got a bargain,' Brady said. 'He'll plug the bullet-holes and iron out the dents, give it a lick of paint and the price will go up to four hundred dollars again.'

'I know. But he had us over a barrel and he knew it. We had to be rid of the car.'

'And the gun?'

'I couldn't take it with me. You know very well they don't let you travel in airliners these days with guns in your baggage.'

'As long as they let us travel at all, I'll be satisfied. I won't feel safe until we're out of this country and on our way back to dear old England.'

'Patience, Steve darling,' she said. 'Patience.'

They were lucky. They were able to get seats on a flight out the next morning. Brady was on edge while they waited to board the plane, and again when they were in their seats and it was still on the ground. When it was finally airborne he breathed a sigh of relief.

'Were you worried?' Linda asked.

'Worried!' he said. 'Whatever makes you think that?'

Chapter Twenty-Three

HER PLACE

Mr Lessing was practising his putting on the carpet of his office when they were ushered into his presence. Mr Forder was apparently again out on business and Lessing was holding the fort.

'Ah!' he said. 'Here you are. Do sit down.'

He already knew that their mission had ended in failure. Linda had reported by telephone as soon as they arrived in London the previous day, though she had not gone into any detail. She had discussed with Brady the question of just how much they ought to reveal to Adsum and had come to the conclusion that the less said about certain aspects of the operation, the better.

Lessing put the putter and ball away and sat down on the other side of his desk.

'So it didn't pan out, eh? Well, some you win and some you lose. That's life.'

He seemed remarkably unconcerned, Brady thought. He just hoped Adsum was not the kind of firm that paid its agents purely on results.

'That feller, Garfield,' Lessing said. 'Always had my doubts about him. Not quite the type. Killed, you say?'

'Yes,' Linda said.

'Accident with a gun, was it?'

'Something of the sort.'

Only of course there had been nothing accidental about it, Brady thought. Far from it. But he said nothing.

'Dangerous things, guns,' Lessing said. 'Need handling with care.' He turned to Brady. 'Pity you had to be in on a stinker. Not all like that, I assure you. Soon be out of business if they were. Still, I daresay you found it interesting.'

'Very much so.'

'Yes, well, sorry we can't offer you a permanent job with us, but you know the way it is. Of course if at any time we are in a position to throw something your way and you're still available, we'll be in touch.'

He turned again to Linda. 'You'll be putting in a full report for the file, of course. No hurry. Take a few days off. Nothing urgent on the books. Miss Bates will see to the, ah, pecuniary side of things as you go out.'

It was a dismissal. They heard the click of putter on ball even before the door was fully closed behind them.

'Your place or mine?' she said.

He thought about it for a few moments. Then: 'Yours, I think. I'd like to retain happy memories of it now that this thing is getting towards its end.'

She lifted a questioning eyebrow. 'Does it have to be the end?'

'Well, doesn't it?' he said.

'Oh,' she said, 'you never know, do you?'

And then he grinned and said: 'No, you don't, do you?'

'So let's go,' she said.
'Yes,' he said, 'let's do that.'
So they went.
To her place.